A Nordic Knight

and his

Spanish Wife

♡ Kris
Tualla

Kris Tualla

A Nordic Knight and His Spanish Wife is a work of fiction. Names, characters, places and incidents are products of the author's imagination or are used fictitiously and are not to be construed as real. Any resemblance to actual events, locales, organizations, or persons, living or dead, is entirely coincidental.

Published in the United States of America.

© 2015 by Kris Tualla

ISBN-13: 978-1523351510
ISBN-10: 1523351519

*This book is dedicated to the sane people
who surrounded King Henry VIII,
and who survived the actions of
a monarch run amok.*

God works in mysterious ways.

Enjoy!

Chapter One

February 3, 1520
London, England

Jakob Hansen laughed so hard his eyes were tearing. "That is rich, Percy. Stop! I cannot catch my breath."

Sir Percival Bethington, loyal knight in service to King Henry the Eighth, and His Royal Highness's most trusted representative at the Order of the Golden Fleece, crossed his arms over his massive chest.

"I am not making a jest, Jakob."

Jakob, himself a knight in service to Queen Catherine of Aragon, and husband of nearly one year to Her Highness's chief lady-in-waiting, Lady Avery Galaviz de Hansen, wiped his eyes. "Am I to believe that you actually *are* getting married?"

Percy nodded. "I am."

"Good Lord, man—why?" Jakob shook his head and spread his hands. "You have lived for these three decades happily unencumbered by a wife. Has my recent state of bliss influenced you so?"

Bethington stroked his beard. "It is quite true that I have thoroughly enjoyed my singular state. And that you, my friend, are unusually giddy for a Norseman."

"And your exploits with the fairer sex are legendary!" Jakob rested his hands on his hips and drew a deep breath. "Will you give that up willingly?"

Percy shrugged a little. "I am afraid I must."

An unhappy thought occurred. "Do not tell me you have been caught."

Percy's face flushed. "It is not *only* that."

Jakob's shoulders slumped. "Percy—how can you be certain the babe is yours?"

"She was a virgin when I took her to bed."

Jakob looked askance at his friend. "Are you certain of that? There are womanly tricks to make a man believe so, you know."

Percy wagged his head. "Jakob, as you said yourself my exploits are legendary. I am not an ignorant squire when it comes to bedsport. I know a virgin when I bed one."

"Why did you do it, Percy?" Jakob clapped his friend on the shoulder. "Why take her virginity when so many experienced women are eager to join you?"

The knight's face flushed darker. "She has my heart, Jakob. I am smitten."

"Love?" Jakob was stunned. "You love the girl?"

"More than I thought possible." Percy allowed his first smile of the conversation. "She is completely captivating."

Stunned, Jakob tried to picture the women he had seen Percy with of late. "Do I know her?"

"Perhaps. She is the daughter of Lord Basil Woodcote, Earl of Oxford. We met at Windsor last summer, and then reacquainted ourselves during the Saint Nicholas festivities."

Jakob huffed a laugh. "Two months past? You wasted no time, my friend."

"I could not risk another man claiming her, Jakob."

Jakob felt a niggling of recollection. "Describe her to me."

Percy laughed. "She is the antithesis of me. Petite of frame, curling blonde hair, and only nineteen."

Jakob nodded. "I believe I do know the girl…"

"Ah, but if you looked into her eyes, Jakob." Percy sighed. "They are the purest, palest blue you could imagine, framed with the eyelashes of an angel."

Jakob smiled at his friend; Percy was, indeed, captivated. To the point of waxing poetic. That was the last thing Jakob ever expected to hear from his English friend.

Percy pointed a insistent finger at him. "She sees my very soul, Jakob. She knows every misdeed, every misstep, and yet she loves me even so."

"If that is true, then she will elevate you to heights you never imagined possible." Jakob's heart warmed at the thought of his own wife. "Just as Avery has done for me."

"And you for her, if we are to be honest." Now Percy clapped Jakob's shoulder. "I have hopes that Anne and I can achieve what you and Avery have."

"Have you talked to Henry yet?" Jakob asked.

Percy nodded. "Henry gave his permission three days past. And I have returned last night from Oxford where I received her father's blessing."

Jakob was still adjusting to this completely unexpected shift in his best friend's situation. He could not wait to tell Avery and see what her reaction would be. He wondered if his wife had any clue through her connections in Catherine's court, or if this engagement would be news to everyone.

"When will you marry?"

"The banns will be read today. So the wedding mass will be in three weeks." Percy tilted his head. "Will you stand with me, Jakob? As I did for you?"

"Of course!" Jakob grinned. "I would be honored."

§ § §

Avery left Queen Catherine's presence when her husband beckoned her into the Tower of London's wide upper hallway. "Is something amiss?"

Jakob's dark blue eyes twinkled with amusement. "That depends on your interpretation."

Avery folded her arms. "What has occurred?"

"Percival Bethington is getting married."

Avery smacked her husband in the chest. "Oh, stop that. Be serious."

"I do not jest," Jakob declared. "The man is smitten."

Her forehead furrowed. "By whom?"

"The Earl of Oxford's daughter."

Avery gave a little gasp. "Anne Woodcote?"

Jakob's brows shot upward in surprise. "Do you know her?"

"Yes!" Avery started to laugh. "And *she* is the girl Percy will marry?"

Jakob looked suddenly uncomfortable. "Why is this funny?"

"Because Anne spits fire, Jakob." Avery tried to imagine Percy with the deceptively petite and pale young woman. "She is not one to be trifled with."

"It seems he did trifle with her…" Jakob gave her a knowing look.

"Ah." This engagement was making sense now. "She is with child."

"Yes."

Avery smiled and shook her head. "Then I assure you that she chose him. Not the other way around."

Jakob seemed to ponder that. "He says she is attractive."

"She is more than that. She is beautiful," Avery agreed. "And well liked, in case you were worried."

"She must know of his reputation," Jakob posited. "He claims that she does."

"I am certain that she does. Perhaps that is why she chose to seduce him." Avery laid her hand on her husband's chest and looked up into his eyes. "A man who has lived life is always more interesting."

Jakob bent down and kissed her softly, then rested his forehead against hers. "And a wise and beautiful wife who knows what she wants is a blessing."

"I love you, husband, and wish we could dally longer, but I

must return to Catherine." Avery gave Jakob a quick kiss. She turned to the door but looked back over her shoulder. "Has Henry approved?"

"Yes. As well as the Earl."

Avery grinned. "I cannot wait to discuss this with Catherine."

§ § §

Jakob left the Tower and walked toward the house in which he and Avery lived. Built inside the walls of the ancient fortress, the house was one in a long row of private residences which housed high ranking guards and married couples in service to the royal couple.

The damp winter air in London always made his damaged thigh ache, but Jakob avoided taking opium until the pain was unbearable. Happily, sharing a bed with his wife warmed him through the night and he awoke much less sore than when he was a bachelor.

He opened the door and stepped into the small drawing room, immediately feeling the welcome warmth from the fire on this chilled winter's day.

Askel popped his head through the open door to the kitchen. *"Hva kan jeg gjøre for deg, min herre?"*

His loyal valet, Askel, had followed Jakob from Denmark to England to Spain, then back to England, on to Norway, and again to Denmark, before returning to England to settle down for good.

"English, Askel," Jakob chided. "We live here now."

The valet heaved a sigh. "What will I do for you, my lord?"

Jakob dropped into a chair. "I have news."

"What sort of news?"

Jakob flashed a crooked smile. "It seems that Sir Bethington has decided to marry."

"Yes." Askel's head bobbed. "And?"

Jakob frowned. "Are you not surprised?"

Askel shook his head. "Denys tells me yesterday."

Bethington's valet was Askel's first friend in England, and the two younger men grew to trust each other as much as their employers did.

"Why did you not tell me?" Jakob asked.

"He tells me not to."

Jakob quirked a brow. "You make me question your loyalty, Askel."

The valet laughed. "I serve you all over the world."

"You are lucky that I have taken you all over the world," Jakob countered.

Askel shrugged. "He says Bethington tells you today."

Avery's maid Emily came into the drawing room. "Can I get you anything, my lord?"

Jakob turned his head to face her. "Did you know that Sir Bethington is getting married?"

Emily blinked, her expression puzzled. "The same Sir Bethington who pursued Lady Avery so intently, and then went to Spain with you?"

Jakob nodded. "That is the one."

Emily's regard slid to Askel. "Is this a jest?"

Askel grinned at her and patted his belly. "No. The lady has a baby."

Emily appeared properly horrified. "Is he being forced by the king?"

"Not at all." Jakob wagged his head and smiled. "It seems the intrepid knight has been irrevocably felled by love."

§ § §

Catherine laughed so hard that Avery feared for the queen's ability to breathe.

"Of all the men at court, I thought Percival would be the most careful." Catherine gasped for air. "To be caught by a virgin? That is too delicious."

"I told Jakob that Percy was actually the victim." Avery smiled. "But apparently he was quite a willing one."

"I needed a laugh today." Catherine's expression sobered.

"My course has started right on time."

Avery squeezed her friend's hand. "Do not give up hope, Cathy. You are still young enough."

The queen shook her head. "Henry is besotted with Bessie's son, and I fear he is still warming her bed."

And that's why Henry did not tell Catherine about Percival's engagement.

Avery gave Catherine a sympathetic look. She did not dare ask how often Henry was visiting Catherine—that was a step too far, even for her. When the queen of one of the most powerful countries in the world was involved, even lifelong friends must maintain a certain level of decorum.

Since returning to London last year Jakob refused to continue to pretend to be the king, in spite of the striking resemblance between the two men. It was a moot point in any case, because Catherine found out about his affair with Bessie once Jakob left for Spain. She miscarried soon after.

And when Henry stepped forward and claimed Bessie's son as his child, there was no reason for the king to hide his continued extra-marital relations with her any longer.

"When will the wedding take place?" Catherine asked.

"As soon as the banns are read."

"The wedding will be a pleasant diversion." Catherine leaned toward Avery. "Every man and woman who knows Percival will be in attendance, and betting on whether or not he actually goes through with it."

Chapter Two

February 10, 1520
The North Sea

The trade ship *Albergar* bucked over the waves on its way from Arendal, Norway to the ports of London. This journey was a continuation of the ship's maiden voyage and she was holding up well, even with the rough seas and a hold filled with goods.

A deck hand stuck his head into the purser's cabin. "Mister Esteban, the captain wants to see you."

"Tell him I will be right there." Gonzalo closed his cash drawer and turned the key. Pushing his stool back he stood, pocketed the key, and strode out of the cabin.

Captain Montero sat at his desk conversing with the boatswain, a man Gonzalo didn't care for. While the boatswain was in charge of the deckhands, he seemed to feel that Gonzalo fell under his authority as well.

"I answer to the captain, and only the captain," Gonzalo reminded him more than once. "So leave me be."

Gonzalo knocked on the open cabin door. "You wished to see me, Captain?"

Captain Montero turned to face him. "Mister Esteban. Come in."

"I shall be on my way, then." The boatswain spun on his heel and walked past Gonzalo without meeting his eyes.

Gonzalo stepped forward. "How can I be of service, sir?"

"We are making decent progress in spite of the weather." Montero tapped on the map spread across his desk. "I expect we will reach the mouth of the Thames by sunrise tomorrow."

"And dock in London by nightfall?"

The captain nodded. "How are our numbers?"

"We stand to make a decent profit, sir, even after we restock our supplies for the long journey back to Barcelona."

"Good."

"When will you want to hand out the pay packets?" Gonzalo assumed the sailors would not be paid when they docked, but only after their cargo was unloaded and stored in a warehouse.

"Have them ready before we reach London so we can pay them as soon as the work is finished." Montero's mouth twisted into a knowing grin. "Arendal was a small port and I am afraid many of the men found the, ah—*amenities*—lacking. They will be eager to sample the vast entertainments of London."

Whores and taverns.

Gonzalo Esteban was careful to stay away from both. "Yes, sir."

"That is all. You are dismissed."

"Thank you, sir."

As he made his way back to his cabin, a sly smile curled his lips.

At long last, I shall have my rightful reckoning.

§ § §

Eleven months had passed since Avery took possession of the trade ships built with her dead husband's money, and five since the first ship set sail according to the letters from her

Barcelona business partner, Señor Gustavo Salazar.

Once the *Albergar* docked in London, the sale of its cargo should raise enough cash for Avery to repay the money which Catherine so generously loaned her in her darkest hour.

"And that ship should arrive sometime this month," she told Jakob over breakfast in their bedchamber. "After stopping in Arendal, of course."

"Johan was very optimistic about trading with Spain," Jakob said about his elder brother. "I confess to being curious as to what sort of goods he was able to provide."

"He mentioned fish," Avery recalled. "Arctic salmon, cod, herring. Pelts and wool. Even ice, I believe."

Jakob rubbed his belly. "I would love some fresh salmon right now."

Avery considered her very handsome husband. "Do you think that Johan will ever marry again?"

Jakob shrugged. "I cannot say. After so many years apart, I am afraid I do not know my brother well enough anymore."

Avery reached over and laid her hand over his. "I am sorry, Jakob."

"It was my choice to leave Arendal, Avery." He gave her a wan smile. "And I am glad that I was able to see my mother and my brothers this past year at last."

Avery sipped her tea. "Catherine's mood has been sour. She is not with child yet again."

Jakob shook his head. "The talk among the men is that Henry stopped visiting her bed once Bessie's boy was born."

"I feared that was the case. I cannot ask her outright, of course." Avery nibbled some smoked fish, considering her own childless situation.

In her case, never conceiving with her horrid first husband was a blessing. And at thirty-six years of age she did not want to bear a child. She told Jakob this before they married and thankfully he was of like mind. Now the couple used precautions to assure that they were not unhappily surprised.

"She does have Mary, who will be queen someday," Jakob observed. "And the girl has a keen mind for a four-year-old."

"That must be her solace, then." *And I will need to remind her of that fact.* "How are Percy's wedding plans coming?"

Jakob chuckled. "Henry is turning this into one of his celebrations."

Avery grinned; Henry was always in favor of a social gathering. "Will there be a theme?"

"Valentine's of course. Even if the actual ceremony will be ten days or so after the date, Henry says that the entire month of February celebrates romance." Jakob chuckled again. "And what is more romantic than the epitome of the gay bachelor being tamed into marriage at long last?"

February 11, 1520

Avery sat with Catherine, who was ordering new gowns for herself and Princess Mary in anticipation of Percy's wedding feast.

"She is old enough to be presented as the future queen," Catherine explained. "I must not allow circumstances to distract Henry from his daughter's rightful position."

Avery agreed. "Not that any bastard could ever claim the throne."

Catherine shot her a fierce look. "No, the Pope would never allow the issue of an adulterous affair to be crowned as king—or queen should it come to that—of a loyal Catholic nation."

"Lady Avery?" A page stood at the door.

"Yes?"

"A messenger has brought this for you." The man held out a folded paper. There was no seal.

"Bring it to me, please." Avery shifted a bolt of velvet from her lap and accepted the note.

Catherine watched her expectantly. "What is it?"

Avery gasped with joy. "My trade ship has begun its journey up the Thames!"

Catherine beamed at her. "Then it should dock by nightfall."

"And I shall be able to repay you within a fortnight." That

was an enormous relief; Avery hated owing anyone money, even her closest, richest, and most powerful friend.

Catherine picked up a sample of lace and held it against a bolt of red and black brocade. "This is the ship that sailed to Norway, isn't it? What's it called?"

"The *Albergar*." Avery flashed a sly smile. "The name served me very well, so I chose to revive it."

§ § §

Jakob accompanied his wife to the London dock just before the sun set. "We will not stay long," he warned. "This is not a safe place at night."

Avery opted not to mention the nighttime forays she enjoyed for years. Passing herself off as a man to passersby, she met with a young whore named Lizzy who kept her informed of rumors and scandals involving the Tudor court. If Avery discovered anything of import she would tell Catherine the next day.

Catherine never asked Avery how she knew what she knew, but the queen soon discovered that Avery's stealthy intelligence was usually quite accurate.

"Thank you for accompanying me, Jakob." Avery leaned her back against his chest, in part because of the damp and chilled air. "I am far too excited to sit quietly in our home this night."

She felt his chest bounce with amusement. He leaned down and spoke in her ear. "I confess to being very curious as well."

His warm breath tickled the skin on her neck in a very pleasant manner.

"I may not be able to fall asleep easily after such excitement," she murmured. "I might require a diversion."

"At your service, my love," he replied and kissed her neck. "Whatever diversion you require, I shall happily provide."

Once the ship was secured against the dock with thick ropes, the wide and heavy plank was lowered into place. Men began to scramble up and down, carrying bundles and crates as they did.

"The majority of the goods will be dealt with tomorrow in the light of day," Jakob explained. "What they are transferring now are the personal effects of any crew or passengers who are disembarking."

"Hello, there." The feminine voice to Avery's side was familiar and welcomed.

Avery smiled at Lizzy. "How are you doing?"

The whore shrugged and flashed a crooked grin. "I have no complaints."

"Is anything of interest going on?"

"Bethington's marriage is gaining the interest of the bookmakers." Lizzy leaned forward and looked up at Jakob. "The odds are now three to one that he will not show up."

"I might take that," Jakob teased.

Avery elbowed her husband in the belly.

Lizzy smiled. "I will move along, my lady. I do not wish to draw unwanted attention to you."

"You know you can always give a message to Higgins if you want to see me." The Tower guard with a penchant for ladies' undergarments was the third person out of the only three who knew about Avery's covert actions.

Lizzy dipped her chin and sashayed toward the disembarking sailors. "Hoy, boys. Lookin' for some comp'ny?"

Avery sighed. "She has too much intelligence to be selling herself like that."

"Unfortunately, opportunities and intelligence are not gifted in tandem," Jakob observed. "As is evident in any royal court, as you are keenly aware."

That reality was unfortunate but, "True."

The few passengers aboard were beginning to disembark. "Shall we return to the Tower?" Jakob asked. "We can return in the morning to speak with the captain."

"I suppose." Avery turned to face Jakob. "I am becoming a bit chilled."

He was not looking at her. He was staring at the ship like he could not believe what he saw.

"Jakob?"

He shook his head and grabbed her hand, pulling her toward the bottom of the plank. She hurried to keep pace with his limping but lengthy stride. Jakob halted in front of a tall woman whose faded red hair was heavily streaked with white. She looked at Jakob. Even in the dimming evening, Avery could see the blue of her eyes was ringed in white. An astonished smile spread the older woman's cheeks. "Jakob!"

"Bergdis?" Avery yelped. "What are you doing here?"

"*Mor, hvor er du her?*" Jakob asked in Norsk.

Jakob's mother reached for her son's hands. "*Jeg har kommet for å besøke min kjære sønn og hans vakre kone.*"

Avery remembered enough of the language to understand the simple sentence: I have come to visit my dear son and his beautiful wife.

Chapter Three

Gonzalo Esteban stood near the rail of the *Albergar* and watched the old woman walk down the gangplank. If his luck held, he would recognize the man or woman who met her at the pier.

When she boarded the ship in Arendal, the name Hansen caught his immediate attention. He would have asked her outright about her family if he could have, and he was certain any interest he showed in her would have been welcomed. But Bergdis Hansen sat alone at meals and walked along the deck alone these last weeks.

The reason, of course, was that the woman only spoke an unintelligible language than sounded nothing like his elegant Spanish. And though Gonzalo was working on his English, that was of no help either. He managed to communicate a few details with her using what bits of Latin he remembered from church, combined with hand motions and pantomime.

Gonzalo saw the tall Nordic knight and his haughty Spanish

bitch of a wife walking toward the ship. He pulled the brim of his hat lower and watched them like a hawk watches its prey. As Bergdis made her cautious way down the steep plank, the knight grabbed his wife's hand and pulled her to meet the old woman.

By the look on his face, he had no idea she was coming.

Gonzalo narrowed his eyes and intently watched the exchange. Bits of translated conversation drifted upward, carried by the excited surprise of the unexpected visitor.

When the knight had procured a wagon for the woman— who obviously was his mother, judging by her age and the pair's physical similarities—Gonzalo walked down the plank with the lapels of his coat pulled up and the brim of his hat still pulled down. Once the trio was on their way, Gonzalo followed the wagon on the short journey to the fortress's bridge across a putrid moat. Staying on the city's side, he watched the couple pass through the massive guards' gate at the Tower of London without being questioned.

He allowed himself a grim smile, then. His task would not be an easy one, but Gonzalo was a determined man. He had been deeply wronged, and that wrong must be set to rights.

"Enjoy your night, Hansen," he muttered into the fog as he returned to the ship.

You have no idea what else is coming.

§ § §

By the time Jakob translated his mother's answer for Avery—*I have come to visit my beloved son and his beautiful wife*—gathered his mother and her trunk, and hired a wagon to deliver them to his house inside the Tower walls, the sun had fully set and a cold foggy darkness enveloped the city.

Jakob was completely stunned to see his mother disembark from the trade ship; in her lifetime the woman had never traveled as far as Christiania, where Akershus Festning protected Norway's capitol city. When she walked down the gangplank of Avery's ship here in London, he could not believe his eyes.

But he had the good sense to get her out of the cold and into their cozy house, and ask their cook to serve some warmed stew and hot bread before demanding to know what she was doing here.

Avery poured Bergdis a glass of wine. "My Norsk is bad," she said apologetically in that language. "But I think your son *has* none."

Jakob startled; he was not aware his silence was so obvious amidst the hustle of getting his mother situated in his home.

"Mamma, your appearance has both pleased and surprised me. But I *am* at a loss for words." Jakob accepted the glass of wine which Avery poured for him as well. "Please tell me what prompted you to do such a thing."

Bergdis glanced at Avery. "Do you understand?"

She smiled and gave a little shrug. "A little. Jakob talks me after."

Bergdis nodded and returned her attention to Jakob. "When you came to see us last summer, I was so impressed by all that you have done. You took a very bad situation and built a very successful life upon it."

Jakob felt his cheeks warming. "Thank you, Mamma."

"My son walks among kings." She shook her head. "I never imagined such a thing."

"I actually serve Her Majesty, Queen Catherine of Aragon now, as Avery does as her chief lady-in-waiting," Jakob corrected. "But I do converse with King Henry on many occasions."

"Jakob fights Henry in games," Avery managed with a grin. "Jakob does not win and Henry is happy."

Jakob laughed. "Yes, Mamma, I do allow the king to best me, though he is a formidable opponent and often wins by his own skill."

Bergdis' expression brightened. "Might I see some of those games?"

Jakob shrugged. "That depends on how long you stay."

Bergdis looked uncertain. "I do not have my plans made," she admitted. "It was enough of a new experience for me to come to you."

"I am so happy that you did," Jakob said. "But who is taking care of Johan?"

Bergdis shifted her gaze to Avery. "Johan saw how happy your wife has made you. Not long after you left us he decided to court one of the widows in Arendal."

"Did Johan marry?" Avery asked. His wife was clearly following more of the conversation than he thought she could.

"Yes." Bergdis grinned. "She has one daughter, Karin, and she helps Maris run the house. So now Johan does not need me, and I am freed from the responsibility."

"A man always needs his mother." Jakob regarded his aging mother with new eyes. "That is why I wrote my letters to you."

Bergdis reached for his hand. "You know what I mean, Jakob. My tasks are finished. I do not have to work hard any longer."

Jakob considered his mother's hand, its blue veins and long, thin bones visible. "So you decided to board a ship."

Bergdis laughed and waved her hand toward Avery. "Yes. This was Avery's ship, and it was sailing to you. I thought to myself, if my son can travel all over the world, then I can too."

"Johan—was he happy with this?" Avery asked.

"No. When I told him I was going to sail for London, he tried to stop me. But I reminded him that Jakob sailed away as a very young man, and that I could do so as an old woman." She chuckled again. "Your father was not the only stubborn person in that house."

"And here you are." Jakob felt his throat thicken. "I was not certain I would ever see you again, Mamma."

"I could not allow that, Jakob," she murmured. "We have already missed so much, you and I." She turned to Avery. "And I want to know this amazing woman you married."

Avery smiled softly. "You are welcome here for long time."

The thought occurred to Jakob that his mother might never return to Norway. He would ask Avery later if she thought the same thing—and what that meant to them as a couple.

"Yes, Mamma. You are welcome in our home for as long as you wish to remain."

§ § §

Avery sighed and rested her naked body along his. Post coital bliss still thrummed through his core and he held her close, waiting for his heartrate to slow and his breath to return to a normal rhythm.

"*Å min gud,* I am your captive, wife," he mumbled. "Helpless against your assaults."

"I am the victim, Jakob." Avery ran her palm over his chest. "You take me outside of myself, and I am afraid someday I might die of it."

"Never." He kissed her forehead. "I would not allow it."

He heaved a contented sigh and spoke of the other thing which was on his mind. "I never imagined my mother would appear with your ship."

"Nor did I!" Avery leaned up on an elbow and grinned at him. "What a happy surprise."

"It is indeed."

"And now we know about Johan. I am glad that he is not alone." Avery's brows pulled together. "Do you believe your mother felt pushed out of her home by his new wife?"

Jakob chuckled. "You remember that she hid my letters from my father for nearly ten years. My mother is indeed as stubborn as she claims."

"I suppose it does take a strong woman to board a ship and sail to an unknown country, even if the ship is owned by her daughter-in-law, and her son lives at the destination." Avery's expression shifted from concern to curiosity. "Do you think she will ever go back?"

Jakob was always amazed that his wife was able to voice his own thoughts so accurately. "And if she does not?"

Avery smiled. "I would be happy to have her with us for the remainder of her days. As she said, you have missed so much already."

Jakob was surprised. "You understood that?"

"Mostly I understood her mood. A few words here and there confirmed what I thought she might be saying." Avery blew a sigh. "I will need to practice my Norsk. I did not anticipate ever speaking it again."

"My mother also speaks Latin," Jakob reminded her. "And I expect that she will learn English if she chooses to remain here."

"We shall be fine." Avery planted a kiss on his lips. "In the meantime, we do have you to translate for us when we are flummoxed."

"Should I invite her to live with us now?" Jakob asked. "Or should I wait a bit?"

Avery considered that question for a moment. "I think you should tell her now that, once she has had a *chance* to experience our life here in the Tudor court, *if* she wishes to remain in our home she is very welcome to do so."

That was wise advice. "That way, she is free to make either decision at a later date."

Avery nodded. "Yes. And not be forced to decide now, and possibly regret it later."

Jakob frowned. "What might she regret?"

Avery chuckled. "The amount of time we spend in service to the queen? The damp English weather? The crowded, dirty, and noisy conditions in London? Or even the stench of that rancid moat outside."

"It is true that living here is nothing like living in Arendal," he agreed. "But the weather here, though damp, is milder than Norway's. It will go easier on her bones, I think."

"Then it is settled." Avery kissed him again, more slowly this time, before tucking her head under his chin.

Avery always laid on Jakob's right side and he felt her warmth ease the ache in his thigh. He knew she did so purposefully.

Thank you, God, for this woman.

He smiled. *And for bringing my mother safely to us.*

Chapter Four

February 12, 1520

"I am as nervous as a schoolgirl," Bergdis moaned. "Are you certain that I am properly dressed?"

"Yes, you look beautiful," Jakob assured his mother. "Now come with us and meet our employer."

"You mean meet the Queen of England," she grumbled.

Jakob stepped outside his home and walked across the Tower yard with his mother on one arm and his wife on the other. He noticed the curious looks they garnered—some surreptitious and some obvious.

Inside the Tower they encountered Percival Bethington. The English knight's expression shifted from frantically harried to relieved calm once he spied Jakob.

"Thank God you are here, man."

Jakob opted not to introduce his mother at that moment. "Is something amiss?"

"My darling Anne has fallen under Henry's spell and

grasped his suggestion for our wedding ball's theme with great enthusiasm," Percy grumbled. "She insists I have a new tunic made and purchase new hose to match."

"What about your boots?" Avery asked. "Or a hat?"

Percy's horrified gaze shifted to hers. "Do not even mention those things!"

Jakob turned to his mother and translated what had just occurred. When he did so, Percival seemed to suddenly realize that this was not some random woman on Jakob's arm.

"Forgive my rudeness, Madam." He gave Bergdis a royalty-worthy bow. "I am Sir Percival Bethington, knight in service to His Royal Highness, King Henry the Eighth."

Avery stepped forward. "May we present Lady Bergdis Hansen of Arendal, Norway?" She paused, grinning. "She is Jakob's mother."

"Mother?" Percy's brows flew upward. "You said nothing of her visit. Or did you? I confess to being otherwise occupied of late…"

Jakob chuckled. "My mother's arrival yester eve was a complete surprise, Percy, but a very happy one."

"She boarded my trade ship in Arendal, I believe on a sort of whim, and sailed here," Avery explained. "Jakob's older brother remarried and brought a mother and daughter into her house, and they have assumed the management of Hansen Hall."

Jakob did not translate Avery's statement word-for-word, though he agreed with her assessment of his mother's situation. "We are taking her to meet Catherine now."

"Henry was just with her. If you hurry, your mother might meet both sovereigns." Percy produced a scrap of brocade. "I am off to buy new hose to match this."

Jakob tilted his head. "Have you no second thoughts about this marriage, Percy?"

Percy's features eased. "Not a one, Jakob. And the prospect of raising a son warms me throughout."

Jakob glanced at Avery whose lips were pressed together. Even so, her expression shouted *it could be a girl*. Living so closely with Henry, Catherine, and Princess Mary kept that thought in the forefront of their lives at all times.

Jakob smiled. "Then I shall congratulate you yet again, my friend."

Percy bowed to Bergdis once more, and then strode toward the Tower gate. Jakob continued escorting the pair of dear women on their path toward the queen.

§ § §

Avery entered the queen's chambers first and curtsied in front of Catherine and Henry. When she straightened, she addressed Henry.

"You are clearly in fine health, Your Grace. You look particularly fit this morning."

"I went out riding earlier," Henry replied, smiling broadly. "The sunrise was glorious."

Judging by the hard set of Catherine's mouth, it was likely Henry was riding back to the Tower at sunrise, fresh from some woman's bed. Probably Bessie's.

Avery returned the king's smile. "My husband and I received a surprise guest yester eve. Might I introduce her to Your Graces?"

Henry looked slightly annoyed. "I was just about to take my breakfast. Who is it?"

Catherine's irritated gaze cut to her husband's. "Yes, Lady Avery. Please bring her in."

Avery bowed and turned toward the steward at the chamber door. "Please ask my husband and his mother to enter."

"Mother?" Henry blurted. "Do you mean that Nordic knight has the audacity to own a mother?"

Avery returned her attention to the teasing king. "Indeed he does, Your Grace. And as you shall see, he looks just like her."

Jakob limped into Catherine's chamber with a wide-eyed Bergdis on his arm. "Your Highnesses, may I present the Lady Bergdis Hansen of Hansen Hall in Arendal, Norway."

Bergdis curtsied the way Avery showed her. "Your Graces."

"Will you look at that? He does look just like her." Henry

took a step forward and waited for Jakob to close the rest of the gap. "Welcome to England, my lady."

Bergdis responded with a sentence that Avery caught about half of.

"My mother does not speak English as yet," Jakob said. "But she is honored to meet you both, and compliments the queen on her beauty."

"Thank you, Lady Hansen," Catherine replied as she rose from her chair and stepped forward to address Henry. "I do not wish your Grace to miss his breakfast."

Henry glared at Catherine. "My breakfast will wait for me."

Bergdis said something else, and then looked up at her tall son.

"My mother says that she has heard many tales of the King's power and wise negotiating skills." Jakob rubbed his index finger over his upper lip. "I did tell her about the Treaty of London, Your Grace."

Avery noticed with relief that Henry's displeasure with Catherine seemed to dissipate with the translated compliment. "Tell her I am pleased with her son."

Avery lifted one skeptical brow but dropped it before Henry noticed.

Not so pleased that he balked at handing Jakob off to his queen.

Henry walked past the small group, all of whom bowed or curtsied as he passed without a word of farewell. Once he was gone, Bergdis blurted something about faces.

Jakob nodded and replied before translating for Catherine. "My mother says that I do resemble your husband. She did not believe this when I first told her."

Avery thought the resemblance had faded away, but apparently to fresh eyes it was still solidly there. "Of course, Henry shines brighter," she deferred.

Catherine turned her back to Jakob and Bergdis and made a disgusted face. "His shine is quite tarnished, I am afraid."

Avery did not react and was glad to note that Jakob remained silent as well.

"Jakob's mother is welcome to stay, but Jakob has duties to perform." Catherine reclaimed her seat and looked at Avery. "Do you remember your Norsk?"

§ § §

Gonzalo prowled the streets that surrounded the Tower of London in search of the perfect location to carry out his plan. He needed someplace private, where any loud noises would either not be heard or noticed. Luckily, the area around the docks was filled with taverns and whorehouses, so cries of distress were common and largely ignored.

He could not take a chance on rushing his plans, lest he lose this hard-won opportunity.

For six months he languished in Barcelona without a permanent home, laboring at positions far below his status just to keep himself fed and housed. After what transpired at the Mendoza Palazzo, he was forced to assume a different identity as he plotted his revenge against Avery.

Then, when the first of the two trade ships Paolo contracted for was completed, he presented himself to the newly hired captain as an experienced purser, complete with a forged letter of recommendation.

After that came five miserable months of sailing from Barcelona to Norway, with stops along the southern and western coasts of Spain to purchase items for trade. Gonzalo hid his seasickness as best he could until he finally grew accustomed to the constant roll of the ship. Now he was proud to say he could withstand rough seas with the best of any deckhands.

He was damned if he would sail again, even so.

After I finish here, I will not need to.

Gonzalo spied a house that looked uninhabited. He knocked on the door, and when no one answered he tried the latch. The door swung open on sagging leather hinges and he stepped into a disaster.

Over-turned furniture and broken crockery spoke of the violence that precipitated this building's abandonment, and the stench of rotted food and rat droppings proved that its inhabitants made a hasty exit. Gonzalo walked carefully through the three rooms on the ground floor before climbing the wooden steps to the upper level.

There were three small rooms up there as well, but because none had an open window it was too dark to see what unpleasant surprises they might contain. Gonzalo went back down the steps, thinking that this might be the exact thing he was looking for.

I shall bring a lamp and examine the rooms upstairs to be certain.

When he stepped out the front door, he pulled it shut behind him and decided not to waste time or effort on the leather hinges.

"Looking for somebody?" A rather attractive woman approached him, her scandalous clothes declaring her horizontally-practiced trade.

Gonzalo looked confused and concerned. "Do you know what became of the family that lived here?"

"He's gone to the gaol for debts. Fought them pretty badly when they came to take him, as ye see." She tipped her head to the side. "Were ye kin?"

Gonzalo played the odds. "To the wife."

"Aye, well she high-tailed off with another man. Don't know where." The whore shrugged so that the front of her dress gaped, giving Gonzalo a tantalizing view of two large, firm breasts. "Want t' buy me something to eat?"

He felt a stirring in his groin and refused to think how long it had been since anything but his own hand had given him pleasure. Buoyed by the discovery of this house and the news that the inhabitants were long gone, he agreed to the girl's proposition.

At least she smelled clean. And he liked her perfume. "I will want a nap afterward."

She grinned. "I have a *very* comfortable bed." She looped her arm through his. "My name's Lizzy, by the way."

§ § §

Avery did the best she could to communicate with Bergdis while they and Catherine worked together on Princess Mary's dress for the Valentine's ball following Percival Bethington's wedding to Anne Woodcote.

"I want to meet Anne Woodcote personally." Avery threaded her needle. "I only know her from a distance. And by reputation, of course."

"I can summon her," Catherine offered. "I would like to get to know her a bit better before she nabs our precious Percival."

Precious was not how Avery ever thought of Percy. His months-long and unsuccessful pursuit of her hand was one of the reasons her own reputation as the 'Ice Maiden' of the Tudor court stuck to her so strongly.

Of course, no one knew she ran to Catherine's court for safety after an arranged marriage to a ghastly man who eventually died of syphilis. She declined all propositions in the meantime; she would not risk her salvation for either bigamy or fornication, no matter who pursued her.

"Please do," Avery encouraged. "She might benefit from a little fear of the court, from what I have seen."

Catherine waved one of her other ladies over. "Paper and pen please." When they were supplied, Catherine wrote out a note inviting Anne for tea that same afternoon.

"There is no reason to delay this," she said to Avery after instructing the woman to have the note delivered immediately.

Bergdis' hands rested in her lap and she shook her head. "*Øynene mine er for gamle.*"

Avery remembered that *øynene* meant eyes and *gamle* meant old. She gave Bergdis a sympathetic look and held out her hands.

"*Gi den til meg.*" Give it to me.

She did. "*Jeg beklager.*"

Avery shook her head. "Do not be sorry."

Bergdis managed half a smile.

A side door opened and Princess Mary's nurse entered the room with the four-year-old in tow. "Beg your pardon, Your Grace, but the Princess was asking for you."

A smiling Catherine set her needlework aside and held out

her arms. "Come, my darling."

Mary walked forward very properly until she reached her mother. Catherine pulled her daughter close and kissed her forehead.

"Let her stay a little while, Nurse."

"Yes, Your Grace." The nurse curtsied and settled on a straight wooden chair near the door which she and Mary had entered through.

Mary looked over the pretty fabrics, keeping her fists clutched by her side; she knew better than to start touching things.

Bergdis held out a scrap. "Kom her."

The words sounded the same in English, so Avery repeated them. "Come here. It is the same. *Samme*."

Bergdis lit up. "Same. *Ja*."

Mary looked to her mother for permission.

"Go on sweetheart," Catherine encouraged. "This is Sir Hansen's mother."

Mary faced Bergdis and stepped close enough to claim the fabric. Bergdis patted her lap. Mary nodded. Bergdis lifted Mary onto her lap and began to sing her a song in lilting Norsk, all the while showing Mary how to fold the scrap into a flower.

Avery watched in fascination. The older woman who moments earlier looked defeated by the demands of the fine needlework, now beamed at the future Queen of England and entranced the girl with the magical transformation of a piece of useless fabric.

Bergdis looked up and reached for her needle and thread.

Avery handed it to her. Bergdis sent it through the base of the flower a couple times and then tied a knot. Avery handed her mother-in-law the scissors without being asked.

Mary held up the flower, grinning from ear to ear. "Look, Mother. A flower for me."

Catherine looked loving at her only living child. "Do not forget to thank Lady Hansen for her kindness, Mary."

The girl turned to Bergdis, her expression earnest. "Thank you, Lady Hansen. Will you make me another?"

Chapter Five

Bergdis communicated that she wanted to lie down and rest, so after Mary left her mother's chamber with her nurse, Avery escorted Bergdis back to her and Jakob's house and gave her over to Emily and Askel's competent care.

Askel was more than happy to act as translator for Jakob's mother, which probably had to do with Jakob's insistence that the valet abandon Norsk and become proficient in English.

Anne Woodcote, daughter of the Earl of Oxford, appeared in Catherine's presence promptly at three o'clock. If she was at all nervous appearing before the Queen, she did not show it.

Anne executed a perfect curtsy. "I am honored by your invitation, Your Grace."

Then she turned to Avery and curtsied again. "I am also well pleased to finally meet you, Lady Avery." She straightened. "Percival has told me quite a lot about you and Sir Hansen."

"Come and sit, Anne." Catherine indicated the empty chair near their low table. "We want to get to know the woman who snared our dear Percival's heart."

Avery smiled at the petite blonde. "Unfortunately, Percy has told us little about you in return."

Anne flashed a knowing look. "Other than the reason for our hasty marriage, of course."

Avery recoiled and cut her glance to Catherine's.

"You are overly direct, Lady Woodcote," Catherine chided.

Anne looked unapologetic. "I cannot abide secrets that are not actually secrets. Once I birth an eight-pound son less than six months after the wedding, what will people say then? I would rather be honest now."

"I shall be honest," Avery bristled. "He says you claimed to be a virgin when he took you."

"And I was, my lady. I assure you." Anne winced. "I was swollen and in pain for a week afterward."

Catherine's expression was pensive. "Has he bedded you since?"

"Yes." Anne blushed at that. The deepening pink of her cheeks highlighted the pale turquoise of her eyes and the flaxen color of her hair. The girl truly was stunning.

She lifted one shoulder in a shy half-shrug. "But it no longer hurts."

Though he was thrilled now, Avery tried to imagine how Percival received the news of a baby. Even more so, "What did your father say when he discovered your condition?"

"He was not pleased, and he threatened to castrate Percy." Anne shook her head. "But I told him it was my idea, because I was in love."

Avery and Catherine exchanged a look.

"You are in love with Percy?" Catherine asked.

Anne's demeanor as she answered could only be described as wistful. "Oh yes. He is the most handsome man I have ever met."

Avery agreed that the big, brawny, brunette knight with blazing green eyes and perpetually ruddy cheeks framing an easy grin was an attractive man. Dozens of women had fallen under his charm and into his bed over the years.

Percival Bethington never lacked for female companionship, that was certain.

"How old are you Anne?" Avery asked.

"I will be twenty in two months. And I know that Percy is ten years my senior." A pretty frown formed over her brows. "But that is not unusual."

"No, it is not," Avery agreed. "But you are aware that he has had several... encounters. With women."

Anne's head fell back and she laughed delightedly. "Lady Avery, you are being so sweet to try and spare my feelings."

"So you are aware of his reputation?" Catherine pressed. "A well-deserved one?"

Anne nodded, still smiling. "I am. In fact, Percy does not remember this, but we first met about eight years ago. That was when I decided."

"Decided?" Avery glanced at Catherine. "You were only twelve. What did you decide?"

"To marry him, of course."

That left Avery speechless.

"Does he know that?" Catherine asked.

"I told him, yes. But he does not recall the occasion." Anne shrugged. "And why should he? I was still a child, and there were plenty of grown women present."

Avery shook her head. "This is a most unusual story, I have to say."

"My father says when I set my mind on something, I am like a stallion who has taken the bit in his teeth." Anne flipped one unconcerned wrist. "Gender differences notwithstanding."

The flame of understanding sprung to light in Avery's mind. She looked at Anne with new respect.

"You knew that the only way to make him marry you was to give him your virginity and conceive his child."

Anne waved a finger in denial. "Not the *only* way. He had to fall in love with me first, as deeply as I had with him."

Avery's respect jumped another notch. "So he declared his undying love before you took him to bed?"

"Of course." Anne leaned forward. "I was not so foolish as

to gamble my entire life away before I knew I had the right cards in my favor."

Avery stared at. Catherine. "What do you make of our determined young friend?"

"I must confess that she has orchestrated her circumstances more effectively than many experienced women I know."

"And Percy is truly smitten," Avery admitted. "I have never seen him happier."

Catherine turned her regard to Anne. "I like you. Please visit me more often once you are married."

Anne looked suddenly shy again. "Thank you, Your Grace. I would be pleased to do so."

"I do have one question, though." Avery pinned Anne's gaze. "Percy is certain you will bear a son. What happens if you present him with a daughter?"

"I will not."

Catherine scowled at the girl. "There is no way to be certain. I, of all people, know that well."

Anne dipped her chin. "I mean no disrespect, Your Grace. But a son is what I planned. The babe does not dare to come out unequipped."

§ § §

"She said that?" Jakob roared his laughter. "Catherine must have wanted to rip her head off!"

"*I* wanted to rip her head off!" Avery waited while Emily tied her underskirts over her panier. "And yet in spite of that horrific misstep, the girl is completely engaging."

Jakob looked askance at her. "Truly?"

Avery dove under her overskirt and came out through the narrowed waist. "Truly. Did Percy tell you she decided to marry him when she was only twelve?"

Jakob wagged his head. "He said that she claimed to have met him years ago, but he did not recall it."

Emily tied the skirt's waist snuggly and slipped the matching bodice over Avery's head. "As it turns out, what I said about her being the one who chose him is true."

Jakob pointed a finger at her. "The question is, does she love him the way he believes she does."

"More, I think." Avery drew a deep breath while Emily tied the lacings on her bodice, assuring herself the ability to breathe adequately that evening. "She has devoted her life to becoming his wife."

Jakob stood and looked at his reflection in the tall silvered glass in their large bedchamber. "Do I need to change my tunic?"

"What did you do today?" Avery countered.

"I trained with the squires. But I took it off so it would not become soiled."

Avery leaned close and sniffed. She wrinkled her nose and stepped away from him. "The tunic is fine, but I believe you should change your shirt."

Jakob nodded and opened the door. "Askel! Come give me a hand."

§ § §

Every night that Henry or Catherine was in residence, dinner was served promptly at eight o'clock in the Tower's formal dining room. Jakob and Avery entered the room with Bergdis in tow, in spite of the older woman's objections.

"I do not have the appropriate gowns," she told Jakob. "And I cannot converse with anyone in any case."

"Only this one time, Mamma. Let me show you off." Jakob looped one arm around her shoulders and kissed her forehead. "After tonight, you can dine here with Emily and Askel if you prefer."

Now he watched her face as the magnificence of Henry's court overwhelmed her. Her eyes were round as saucers and never stopped moving as she took in the visual explosion of fine portraits, expensive fabrics and lace, rich foods on pewter platters, decanters of wine, and crockery pitchers of beer.

"I could never have believed this if I did not see it," she murmured. "You could have tried to tell me and I would have said you were dreaming of Heaven."

Jakob chuckled and leaned down to whisper in her ear. "Let us all hope that Heaven is a less fraught place than living under Henry's capricious moods."

Avery let Bergdis sit between herself and Jakob so his mother would never be left out of their conversation, but she leaned over to speak past her to him. "Percival has brought Anne to dinner at last."

Jakob's gaze moved over the crowd until he found his friend. "Now that Catherine has approved of her, he can bring her into their presence I suppose."

"Has Henry met her?"

"I am not certain. But her father has, and Henry would know of her lineage before granting Percy permission to marry her."

Jakob faced his mother and explained their conversation. Bergdis craned her neck to see the couple in question.

Someone clapped him on the shoulder.

Jakob turned around and looked up into Charles Brandon's eyes. The Duke of Suffolk was Henry's one true friend, a man who could press Henry harder than any other man alive. Even so, Brandon was cautious around the King, never pressing too hard.

The Duke's eyes rested on Bergdis. "Who is this enchanting creature, Hansen?"

Jakob rose to his feet. "May I present my mother, the Lady Bergdis Hansen of Hansen Hall in Arendal, Norway." He cleared his throat. "She does not have any English, in case you are wondering why she did not react to your kind words."

Bergdis smiled up at the handsome duke and lifted her hand.

Brandon took it and pressed his lips to her skin. Then he winked at her. Bergdis blushed furiously and actually giggled.

Brandon straightened. "I see the family resemblance clearly, Hansen. Tell your mother you can thank her for your good looks."

"I will, Your Grace." Jakob bowed his head. "Thank you."

Bergdis leaned close to Jakob and whispered in his ear. "I am so glad I came. If only your brothers could see you now."

Chapter Six

February 13, 1520

Avery boarded the *Albergar* to meet with the captain. Jakob wanted to come with her, but she said no.

"Askel can escort me to and from the dock if you are worried for my safety," she conceded. "But I control that captain's employment, and I cannot have my position undermined by looking as though I require my husband's presence in order to conduct my business."

Jakob reluctantly agreed to her logic, charging Askel to watch over her or lose his life by failing.

"Y—yes, my lord." Askel swallowed and faced Avery. "I beg you, my lady, have a care for me."

Avery shook her head. "Jakob is not going to kill anyone. And I am not going to do anything foolish."

Now she was being led to the captain's cabin in the front of the ship and tucked under the main deck. She carried a ledger with her, updated each time her business partner sent her a copy of his accounting. Gustavo Salazar was required to show his balance sheets to her Barcelona accountant every three months since she left Spain and send her a copy as well.

Their agreement was for Gustavo to pay her sixty-five percent of all profits until she earned back the three hundred thousand maravedis which was required to complete the ships— and less than the value of her husband's palazzo, which she deeded to the shipbuilder in exchange for completing her two trade ships.

After that was achieved, she would give Gustavo forty-nine percent ownership of the vessels and sixty percent of the profits. This first sailing was the beginning of fulfilling that dream.

The *Albergar's* Captain Montero was an attractive man in his forties with gray temples and a neat gray-streaked beard. He stood when she entered the bright, windowed cabin.

"Lady Hansen?" He gave her a shallow bow. "I am Captain Juan Montero. It is an honor to meet you."

Avery walked toward him. "And I am pleased to meet you, Captain. Thank you for taking such good care of my ship."

He smiled. "She is a worthy vessel."

Avery dipped her chin in acknowledgement. "I hope you have good news for me."

Montero nodded and indicated a chair. "Have a seat, my lady, and I will show you the numbers."

Avery frowned. "Is the purser not available?"

Montero gave her an apologetic look. "I am afraid Mister Esteban has fallen victim to a common stomach malady and is unable to join us."

Avery felt a jolt of recognition. "Esteban?"

"Gonzalo Esteban. He came from Madrid with very high recommendations."

Avery nodded and forced herself to ignore the similarity between the purser's name and that of the embezzling majordomo of her dead husband Paolo Mendoza's estate—and the man who nearly destroyed her life.

Avery sat in the indicated chair. "Show me your numbers, then. I am very curious to see how we have done thus far."

§ § §

Gonzalo waited nearly an hour into Avery's meeting with Montero before putting his plan into action. The delicate balance between beginning too soon, while there was still much business left to discuss, and too late, which would leave him scant time to complete the arrangements, needed to be perfectly chosen.

The purser walked down the ship's plank to the lady's waiting valet. "I have a message from Lady Avery."

The man straightened and looked at him. "Yes?"

Gonzalo held out a hand with several coins. "The lady wishes you to go to a shop and purchase some paper and ink for her."

That suggestion was met with a deep frown. "I am under orders not to leave my post."

"Your orders have changed, obviously."

He shook his head. "Her husband gives me orders."

This must be Hansen's man, whom he thankfully never met in Barcelona, if indeed this valet had been there.

Gonzalo scoffed. "Shall I go back inside and inform the lady that her requests are not to be honored, but only her husband's?"

"I—" The valet was caught. "But—"

"Fine, then." Gonzalo moved to put the coins in his pocket. "I will tell the lady that you refused her request."

He turned to climb back up the plank when the other man grabbed his arm. "Give me the coins. I will do as she bids."

As soon as the valet turned his back and began to weave his way through the perpetually busy pier, Gonzalo scanned the crowd for his next accomplice.

"You, there!" he called out to a tall man with a blank expression who was sitting on a barrel.

He looked startled. "Me?"

"Yes." Gonzalo approached him. "How would you like to earn some money?"

He squinted at Gonzalo. "How much money?"

The purser held out another fistful of coins, allowing them to gleam dully in the half-hidden sun.

The man's eyes widened. "What I got t' do?"

"Do you know the empty house on the other side of Tower Hill?" Gonzalo asked. "The one where the man was bundled off to gaol and then his wife ran off?"

"Aye."

Gonzalo poured the clinking coins from one hand to the other. "A lady in a blue gown and a fur wrap is going to appear at the top of that ship's plank." He pointed at the *Albergar*. "She will be looking for her valet."

"Aye..."

"You need to tell her that something happened and her man was called to a house across the way." Gonzalo leaned in closer. "Then you say whatever you must in order to get her to follow you to that empty house."

The man scowled. "Why for?"

"That is not your concern."

He rubbed his scruffy chin. "I dunno."

"You can keep the fur," Gonzalo sweetened the pot. "I have no need for it."

Hurry up you fool. Time is wasting.

"Maybe." He tilted his head. "When do I get paid?"

Gonzalo refrained from sighing his relief. Barely. "As soon as you arrive at that house with the lady, all of this is yours."

The man's scowl deepened. "How much is that?"

"Half a crown."

"Bloody hell!" He rose to his feet and looked down at Gonzalo. "And all I got t' do is convince her t' follow me to that house?"

"Yes."

His eyes moved past Gonzalo. "Is that her?"

Bloody hell, indeed.

Gonzalo glanced over his shoulder, praying that she did not see him. Lady Avery was scanning the crowd and she looked extremely displeased. "Yes. Lady Avery."

The man nodded. "I will take her t' that house."

Gonzalo turned his back to the ship. "And I will be waiting for you there."

§ § §

Jakob will be furious.

Avery could not believe that Askel had disobeyed Jakob and left his position at the bottom of the plank. Even if he had to relieve himself, he could have done so over the edge of the pier like all the other men did.

"He better have a good excuse, or I fear for his employment, if not even his life," she muttered into the damp breeze.

A tall non-descript man was moving toward the ship, and he was looking up at her. He called out, "Lady Avery?"

Do not say yes until you know what is going on. "Why do you ask me that?"

He looked apologetic. "I have a message for a Lady Avery who was on this ship. Do ye know where I can find her?"

Avery's pulse surged. "What is the message?"

"Her man has been in a fight."

Jakob? Is that where Askel went?

Avery tugged the fur wrap tighter and began her descent down the plank. "Where is he?"

The tall man shook his head, his scraggly brown hair waving in oily hanks. "Beggin' yer pardon, but are ye the Lady Avery?"

She nodded but did not get too close to the unpleasantly aromatic man. "I am."

"Aye, then. Follow me." He spun on a heel and began to walk toward Tower Hill.

"Excuse me, but can you tell me what happened?" Avery demanded of his back.

He shook his head again, but did not look backward at her. "I was asked to bring ye to him."

Avery lifted her skirts so she could walk faster. "Who attacked him?"

The man glanced back at that. "How do ye know who attacked who?"

"I know my man. My husband." Avery raised her voice. "He is a knight of the Queen."

The tall man stopped of a sudden and Avery nearly collided

with him. "The Queen, ye say?"

Avery lifted her chin and glared at the man. "Yes. Both he and I are under her protection."

"That is very pretty information." He chuckled as he turned around to resume his path. "Very pretty indeed."

Her sense of foreboding deepened. "Why?"

He did not answer her.

The man led her over the hill, past the spot where she used to meet Lizzy on her nighttime excursions. Avery looked around, hoping to find some evidence of a disturbance that would corroborate this man's story, but the city of London appeared undisturbed.

The street in front of them now was lined with houses, most of which were in a state of disrepair. Avery stopped walking.

"Where are we going?" she shouted.

Her escort stopped when she shouted and turned to face her. "It's just that house over there."

His vague wave was unhelpful.

"No, I do not believe my husband is there. I will return to the Tower and send a guard to be certain."

Avery spun around and took several long strides toward the massive fortress. The unkempt man grabbed her arm with a grip like steel and yanked her around to face him.

"Nah. Ye'll come wit' me." He pulled her uncomfortably close to him and flashed a knife. "I do not want t' kill ye."

Avery clamped her teeth together and walked with the man. She believed an opportunity to escape would soon present itself if she just kept her wits about her.

Chapter Seven

The man opened the door to an obviously abandoned house and shoved her inside. The small and grimy windows did not allow much light from the graying day to enter, and at first she couldn't make out the contents of the disordered room.

"What is this?" a second man asked. "Why the knife?"

"She changed her mind about coming wit' me, so I had t' convince her." Avery's escort let go of her arm. "And she told me somethin' very interesting that ye left out."

Avery heard the clink of coins and turned her head toward the sound. Her knees nearly buckled when she recognized the second man in the dim room.

"You!" she snarled. "What foolishness are you about now?"

Esteban Gonzales crossed the musty room. Ignoring her question, and with one hand behind his back, he addressed the tall man behind her.

"And what interesting thing is that?"

"She's worth more than ye offered, I'd say. She's under the

protection of the Queen herself."

Esteban sighed and shook his head. "I am afraid that does not change our original agreement."

"And I'm afeared it does," he replied. "The queen'll pay far more'n half a crown to get this one back."

Esteban looked at the man, pity etched in his expression. "That is not possible, I am afraid."

"Well, I say it is."

"Sadly for you, it is not."

Esteban's right hand appeared and the shot from his pistol nearly deafened Avery. She cried out, clapped her hands over her ringing ears, and crumpled to the filthy floor.

The tall man folded limply onto his face, the back of his head gaping gruesomely.

Avery gaped at Esteban. "You killed him!"

Esteban shrugged. "I had to. I could not have a witness."

In spite of her growing fear, Avery straightened until she was sitting up on her knees and glared at her former majordomo. "Are you going to kill me as well?"

"Not yet." He flashed a smug smile. "I need to regain what was mine."

"Yours?" Avery began to tremble more with rage than fear. "What do you believe to be yours?"

Esteban leaned into her face. "The ships of course, you thieving *bitch*."

Avery was appalled. "*You* are the thief! Every penny you spent, you stole from my husband!"

"I earned that money!" he bellowed. "Have you ever been around someone with syphilis?"

When she did not answer, he stepped closer. "There is nothing genteel about a man whose cock and brain are rotting, I can assure you of that!"

"You were paid for your services," she growled.

"Not nearly enough." Esteban waved his arms around his frame, nearly hitting her. "And then you come prancing in and grab everything out from under me."

He waggled a finger in her face. "And now, I will take it all back."

Avery shook her head. "No you will not."

"Yes I will. And I shall begin by giving you what your ignorant ape of a husband gave me."

Esteban dropped the spent pistol, pulled his arm back, and punched Avery in the stomach so hard that she could not draw a breath.

§ § §

Lizzy heard the pistol shot and bit the heel of her hand to keep from screaming.

Was Lady Avery dead?

Tears blurred her vision as she backed away from the low wall she had crouched behind. Turning toward the fortress, she stood, lifted the hem of her skirt, and ran up and over Tower Hill in its hulking direction.

Only half an hour ago Lizzy had seen Lady Avery walking with a man with whom the lady should not have been keeping any sort of company, so she followed the pair. She saw the man grab Avery's arm and she saw the flash of his blade.

The only thing she could do to help was follow and see where he took her friend.

We are *friends. In spite of our different stations.*

Tears rolled down her cheeks and Lizzy swiped them away.

Please, Higgins. Be on duty.

§ § §

Avery's world went momentarily black. She felt her arms being pulled behind her back and the rough scratch of rope scraped her wrists. A rag was tied over her mouth leaving barely enough room for her to pull air through her nose.

Esteban jerked her to unsteady feet and then hefted her over his shoulder. Her abused belly collapsed under the pressure of his frame and she was again unable to breathe.

The blackness returned along with a pleasant numbness,

which lasted until she was dumped on the rough-planked floor in a smaller room and banged her head.

"Sorry there is no fire. It might get chilly." Esteban laughed. "But do not worry, no one will disturb your evening."

He walked to the wooden door and left the room, closing it behind him.

Avery strained to hear any sounds at all beyond the clump of Esteban's boots on the stairs and the thunk of the front door being forced shut.

At least he hadn't raped her.

Yet.

Avery managed to sit up and tried to push the cloth off her mouth, but because her hands were tied behind her back she couldn't reach her shoulder with her cheeks. She looked around the empty room for any detritus that she could use to cut the ropes binding her wrists: a scrap of metal, a shard of wood, the edge of a stone in the fireplace.

Her stomach hurt from Esteban's assault and a dull ache was forming on the side of her head that hit the floor.

And she was cold. Her fur wrap did not accompany her to this room, apparently. The bastard probably kept it.

Tears stung her eyes.

Do not cry.

Avery would not give that worthless piece of humanity the satisfaction. Instead she scooted across the dusty floor to the cold, sooty fireplace and felt for a sharp rock.

§ § §

"I am looking for Higgins," Lizzy told the guard on duty.

The Beefeater glared down at her. "Get away."

"It's important. It's about—"

"I said get away!" the guard shouted. "Before I have you clapped in irons!"

"You don't understand—"

The guard grabbed her arm and began to drag Lizzy back across the moat's bridge. "I understand what sort of business you do, and we will have none of your type around here!"

He shoved her and she fell to the cobbles, bruising both knees. Lizzy rolled sideways and screamed, "It's Lady Avery! She's in danger!"

The Beefeater waved an annoyed hand in her direction and stomped back into his station.

§ § §

Askel stood in front of Jakob, tears streaming down his pale face. "And so I went to buy the paper and ink."

"Then what?" Jakob asked in Norsk. Askel was far too distraught to attempt telling his tale in English.

"When I returned to the ship, Lady Avery was gone."

Jakob's chest tightened. "Gone?"

Askel nodded. "I talked to the captain—I would not leave the ship until they let me—and he said she never asked anyone to send me on that task."

Skitt.

"What did the man look like?"

"He—he had brown eyes. Dark hair. Almost black. About this tall." Askel held up his flattened hand. "And he had a hat pulled low on his brow."

Jakob scuttled his hands through his hair. Though only four on the clock, the winter sun was on its way toward the horizon. Hazy winter clouds combined with the smoke of countless chimneys and hastened the evening's gloom.

"I have to find her."

"Yes, sir." Askel swiped his wet cheek, leaving a dirty smudge. "I am so very sorry, Sir Hansen. I tried to follow your orders, but the sailor convinced me his message was sincere."

Jakob wanted to grab Askel by the neck and shake the valet until he went limp. He might have if the man had not been so loyal to him for so many years.

"I gave you a task. A simple one, at that," he growled.

"Ye—yes sir."

Jakob dragged his fingers through his hair again. "Damn it!"

Askel gripped his hands in front of his chest so tightly his skin turned alternately white and red. "I will help you, sir. Tell me what to do."

Jakob narrowed his eyes and glared at the valet. "Get my cloak. We are going to the ship."

§ § §

After the Beefeater banished her, Lizzy hurried to the tavern where she regularly took her customers and asked the proprietor to write a note for her.

"Say the Lady A is in trouble," she gave the carefully esoteric wordage. "Tell Sir J that I know where she is."

"Do ye want your name on't?" the tavern keeper asked.

Lizzy thought about that for a moment. Signing the missive was one way to assure that her audience believed her. "Yes," she decided. "Put Lizzy."

Once the note was completed, Lizzy scrawled an X by her name, folded it, and tucked it inside the low décolletage of her dress. "Thank ye, Max. I owe ye a tumble."

He gave her a kind smile. "I will take it."

Chapter Eight

Avery rubbed the rope against the rocks of the fireplace hearth without stopping. Her arms burned with the effort, and she felt blood running over her palms.

The room had a small window but it was shuttered. The winter's early night was falling and she doubted much of the city's lamplight would be able to squeeze past the roughly hung panels. Though she had never been afraid of the dark, she was finding it hard to keep herself from descending into panic at the moment.

Her tongue was dry and rough against the cloth that cut into the corners of her mouth. She was thirsty. And she needed to relieve her bladder.

Pissing on myself would please Esteban, no doubt.

If she had any saliva, she would spit at the thought of his name.

Avery assumed she would be imprisoned here for at least one night. Esteban would need to make his demands, and then allow time for those demands to be met. Or not met.

An unhelpful sob constricted her chest.

Jakob will do anything to save me.

So would Catherine.

Hopefully those were the exact two people which Esteban approached.

§ § §

Lizzy returned to the Tower and settled herself in a dark spot where she could see who came and went from the guard's stone enclosure.

"Come on, Higgins," she whispered. "I need ye this night."

It was too early for the changing of the Tower's gate guards, so Lizzy had no choice but to wait and watch.

When she saw the tall blond man with a slight limp pass under the lamp at the arched entrance to the fortress, she jumped up with a little squeal and ran toward the moat bridge.

"Sir Hansen!" she shouted, drawing the Beefeater's unhappy attention.

He stormed out of his enclosure. "I said stay away, whore!" he bellowed. "Now you're under arrest!"

"Hold!" Jakob's deep voice boomed toward her.

The guard looked back to see who had the audacity to challenge him. "Sir Hansen? What business do you have with this strumpet?"

"I cannot say until I speak with her." Jakob strode past the irate man, his valet hurrying along behind him. "Have you something to say to me, miss?"

He did not use my name.

That was wise. "I have a message for you, Sir, but I weren't allowed to speak to no one about it."

Even in the darkening evening Lizzy could see the knight's face flush with anger. "What is it?"

Lizzy glanced at the angrily huffing Beefeater and handed Lady Avery's husband the note rather than speak her information aloud. "I thought to give it to Higgins."

§ § §

The Lady A is in trouble. Tell Sir J that I know where she is.

Lizzy ✗

"Where?" Jakob growled. He would deal with the ass of a guard later. Right now he needed to find his wife.

"It's not far," Lizzy said. "Just over the hill."

Lizzy lifted her skirts and began to scurry away from the Tower and the angry Beefeater. Jakob's long legs easily kept pace with the girl. Askel was on his own to keep up.

"Tell me what you can," he urged.

"I saw her with a man, a rough sod. That didn't look right." Lizzy was panting a little but did not slow her haste. "Then I saw a knife, and I knew she was in trouble."

Jakob felt punched in the chest. "Did he hurt her?"

"I don't know." Lizzy shook her head. "He took her in an empty house. And I heard a pistol shot."

Oh God, no.

Not Avery.

"Did you go into the house?"

"No, I ran to find Higgins so I could tell him to fetch ye." A hitched sob broke the girl's narrative. "But that Beefeater chased me away. Threatened to put me in irons."

They crested the hill now. A row of houses faced the hill at the bottom. "How did you get this note?"

"I asked someone to write it for me." Lizzy ran the back of her hand under her nose as she stomped down the hill. "Then I went back and waited for anyone who'd help me get it to ye."

Jakob followed Lizzy down the incline, trying to discern in the gloom which house might be the empty one.

The one with no light inside.

"Is that the house?" Jakob pointed at the most likely residence.

"Yes." Lizzy looked up at him. "Do you have a torch?"

Damn.

"No."

Askel produced a thick candle from inside his cloak. "I picked this up this as we were leaving, Sir."

Jakob stared at the valet. "That was good thinking, Askel. For once today, at the least."

He grabbed the candle from the contrite Askel and hoisted himself onto another house's garden wall to light the wick in the streetlamp's fire. Dropping back onto the cobbled street, Jakob winced a little when the shock of the hard landing thrummed up his injured leg.

"I will go inside first," he declared, refusing to acknowledge the discomfort.

When Jakob forced the door open and held the candle up the first thing he saw was the man crumpled on the cluttered floor. The second thing he saw was the gaping hole in the back of the man's head.

"This accounts for the pistol shot, Lizzy" he said softly, silently thanking God that it was not Avery sprawled in front of him. "I recommend you look away."

"I've seen worse," she murmured at his elbow. "Is Lady Avery still here, do ye think?"

Jakob's gaze swept through the room, searching for clues as to what else might have occurred here. "We shall soon know."

§ § §

Avery heard the front door being shoved open. Her head ached, her stomach ached, her tongue was stuck to the cloth tied across her mouth, and her wrists stung painfully with the rope's abrasion. And her bladder was about to burst.

Even so, she had no desire to face Esteban Gonzales again.

Avery carefully scooted away from the hearth lest whoever just arrived discover that she was nearly free of her constraints. Should she lie on her side? Pretend to be sleeping?

No.

Do not appear to be that vulnerable.

Avery considered scooting next to the room's door and trying to trip whoever came through it, but quickly realized that doing so would only anger her captor. Better to act submissive now and wear the rest of the way through her bindings once she was alone again.

Boots on the stairs made her heartbeat skip and her resolve settle.

God be with me.

§ § §

Jakob quickly searched the three rooms on the ground floor before climbing the steep steps to the upper floor. There were three rooms up there, but only one had a closed door.

If the latch had not given way he would have smashed the door off its leather hinges. But it offered up no resistance and Jakob pushed the door wide open. He held up his candle.

A muffled cry emanated from his wife, who was sitting on the floor near the fireplace. Her nearly black eyes were wide below a worried brow. By the light of his candle he saw the reflection of tears.

"Avery!" Jakob was by her side in a blink. He dropped to his knees and untied the rag across her face. "Are you hurt?"

She shook her head and worked her mouth, her tears now streaming down her cheeks. Her breath came in spasms.

"Who did this to you?" he asked, trying to control his rage. "Can you answer me?"

"Esteban."

The painfully croaked name made no sense to him at first. "Esteban? Your majordomo?"

Avery sniffed and nodded. Then she wiggled her bound arms.

Jakob set the fat candle on the hearth and turned Avery to the side so he could reach her hands.

"*Å min gud,*" he murmured when he saw her abraded wrists. "Did he do this to you?"

"No," Avery rasped. "Trying to get free."

Jakob untied the remainder of the rope. "You nearly succeeded."

He helped his wife to her feet. "We shall go home now."

Avery gripped his arm to help her stand. When they reached the steep steps Jakob suggested that she back down after him so he could catch her if she stumbled.

"Lady Avery!" Lizzy gasped. "Thank the Lord!"

Askel crossed himself and looked like he might cry.

Avery was clearly confused by the presence of Jakob's unexpected accomplices.

"How…?"

"Lizzy saw you with the man who brought you here and she followed you," Jakob explained. "Then she came to find me."

That was the easiest explanation for now; a more in-depth one could follow later if necessary, but only after this matter was settled.

Avery reached for Lizzy's hand. "Thank you."

Lizzy looked down at Avery's wrists. "Oh, my lady," she moaned.

"We should leave." Jakob stepped between Avery and the dead man on the floor. "After you, my love."

Avery moved past him and out of the house. Lizzy followed, then Askel, and lastly Jakob. He pulled the front door shut while a plan began to form in his head.

He turned toward Tower Hill and was startled to see his wife squatting at the bottom with Lizzy standing beside her. Askel stood at a short distance with his back to the women. Jakob hurried to Avery's side.

"Was has happened?" he demanded.

Avery rose to her feet slowly, looking embarrassed. "I could wait no longer to empty my bladder, I am afraid," she murmured. "It was use the grass now, or leave a wet trail all the way to the Tower."

Jakob wanted to laugh his relief that no further harm had befallen his wife, unhelpful as that would have been. Instead he said, "If you are ready to continue, I want to get you home so Emily can tend to your wrists."

Avery gripped his arm again. "It was by God's grace that Lizzy saw me, Jakob."

Jakob gave the girl a tight-lipped smile. "Yes, it was."

She leaned closer, and whispered. "Do not be too harsh on Askel, husband. He and I were both taken in by a master of deceit. And it was not the first time."

Jakob laid his hand over hers, gave a reassuring squeeze, and assisted her in the climb up Tower Hill.

No, it was not the first time.

But it will be the last.

Chapter Nine

When the quartet reached the Tower, Lizzy held back. "If it's all the same to ye, Sir Hansen, I'll be on my way."

"Not yet," he said, looking too determined for her to cross. "Stay here."

He sent Lady Avery to their home behind the walls with Askel as a very attentive escort. "Have Emily take care of your wounds. I will be home in short order."

Avery nodded. "Do not dally, husband. I will not feel fully safe until you are with me."

Once she and Askel were inside the far arch, Jakob turned back to Lizzy. "Come with me."

Lizzy had never been inside the gate of the Tower of London and she was not truly eager to go inside now. "Please, Sir…"

Hansen shook his head. "I have a point to make. Come along."

The same guard who threatened her earlier was still on duty, but Higgins appeared in the archway which Lady Avery and

Askel had just passed through.

"Sir Hansen!" he called out. "I have a message for you!"

"Hold a moment," the knight replied.

Jakob took Lizzy by the arm and pulled her in front of the other guard. "Do you remember what this girl said to you when she approached you before?"

"Yes. She wanted Higgins." The guard sneered. "I told her to take her business elsewhere."

Higgins was close enough to overhear them. He looked at Lizzy. "You wanted me?"

Lizzy was not sure she should speak.

"Go on," Hansen urged gently.

Lizzy swallowed her fear and looked up at Higgins. "I wanted ye to carry a message to Sir Hansen for me."

Higgins' brows pulled together. "What message?"

Hansen drew her note from the breast of his tunic. "This message."

Higgins read the note, then handed it to his fellow Beefeater. "And you did not consider this important enough to fetch me?" he growled.

The other guard read the note and blanched. "I never saw this."

"You never saw this because you were a fool," Jakob accused. "You assumed you knew her business when in truth you did not. And your foolishness put the Lady Avery's life in danger."

Higgins' cheeks darkened with fury. "Can you imagine how Queen Catherine will feel when she learns about this? Her chief lady-in-waiting put in danger by your stupidity?"

"I—I am sorry," he stammered.

"You will be plenty sorry, and that's certain," Higgins stated. "Go. You are released from your duty."

Lizzy wanted to stick her tongue out at the retreating Beefeater's back, but refrained. At the least her sense of justice was served.

"And now for you, Lizzy." Sir Hansen's words pulled her attention back to him. He held out his hand. "This is one way that I am able to thank you."

Lizzy held out her palm. She could not believe her eyes when the tall knight dropped three silver coins into it.

"Three quid?" she yelped. "Are ye sure, Sir?"

Hansen chuckled. "If I thought you could keep more without being robbed of it, I would give you more."

"Thank ye, Sir." Lizzy pulled at the neckline of her dress and tucked the coins inside her corset. "I am grateful enough."

"If you ever need anything, Lizzy, please ask." He looked at her kindly. "I do mean that."

Lizzy grinned at the big, handsome man. "I shall always be at your service as well, Sir. And the Lady's."

§ § §

Once Lizzy was on her way, Jakob turned to Higgins. "What message do you have?"

"This." Higgins handed him a folded paper.

Jakob broke the seal and unfolded the brief missive.

Return my ships,
and then I will return your wife.

"The hell I will." Jakob crumpled the note.

Higgins narrowed his eyes. "Is something amiss?"

Jakob considered the Beefeater. "Not for me. But the man who kidnapped my wife and now makes demands will not live to see another sunrise."

"Lady Avery was kidnapped?" Higgins' gaze ricocheted to the path of the retreating guard and back to Jakob. "Bloody hell."

Jakob clapped a hand on the guard's sturdy shoulder. "But I have taken my wife back, and when he returns for her, he will find me in her stead."

"God have mercy on his soul." Higgins chuckled and crossed himself. "Because you, Sir, will not."

§ § §

Avery sat near the fire in the drawing room of the house which she and Jakob were given inside the Tower of London's wall. Emily, her maid, washed Avery's wrists with warm water and a stinging soap, while Bergdis sat nearby. Askel crouched beside Jakob's mother and translated their sparse conversation.

"I have a salve made from oil of lavender and beeswax, my lady," Emily said softly. "It will sooth you and keep the wounds from festering."

"Thank you, Emily." Avery sipped the wine that Emily heated for her with the fireplace poker, and her voice was somewhat restored as a result.

When her husband walked through the door Avery flinched. The look on his face was murderous.

"What has happened?" she asked.

"Do you mean in addition to that thieving liar kidnapping you, binding you, and holding you hostage in a filthy, abandoned house after killing his abettor in cold blood?" Jakob snarled.

Askel murmured into Bergdis' ear and her eyes widened.

Then Jakob pulled the crumpled paper from inside his tunic. "Now he threatens me. He says if I return his ships, he will return my wife."

Avery's indignation surged. "He did not!"

"Oh, indeed he did." Jakob handed her the cryptic note.

"His ships?" Avery looked up at the furious knight, her own rage ignited. "He dares to call them *his* ships?"

Jakob sat in the chair closest to hers. "I am taking this matter to Catherine immediately. But before I do, I want to piece together how this situation came about. Tell me everything that transpired this afternoon."

Avery pulled a steadying breath. "After I arrived at the *Albergar* I examined the ledgers with Captain Montero in his office on the ship," she began. "He said the purser was not feeling well and unable to join us."

"I would place a wager that Gonzales is the ship's purser."

Avery frowned. "How would he procure such a job on one of my ships?"

Jakob shrugged. "It could be easily accomplished by

applying for the position under an assumed name and with someone who did not know his face."

"Of course." Avery's shoulders slumped. "The captain would have hired him, not Gustavo Salazar."

Jakob nodded. "I am certain he did exactly that—with the purpose of searching you out and extracting his revenge. What happened next?"

Avery glanced at Emily who was wrapping her salve-soothed wrists with strips of linen. Her maid told her how distraught Askel was that he had been duped into leaving his post, and she hated to mention it again. But she must.

"When we finished, I went to look for Askel but he was gone." Avery did not dare look at the valet.

"Then the dead man approached you? On the dock?" Jakob pressed.

"Yes. He told me that you were injured and Askel had gone to assist you."

Askel was still translating for Bergdis, and from what Avery could hear he was giving an honest account.

Poor man.

Avery hoped she persuaded Jakob to go easy on his valet— after all, she was as convinced as he was by the tale.

"Did he know Esteban?" Jakob asked.

Avery shook her head. "Based on their brief conversation in my presence, Esteban met him at the dock and offered to pay him to take me to that house. But when we got there, Esteban shot the man instead."

Jakob snorted. "The only witness."

"Yes. He said as much."

Jakob stood. "I am going to speak with Catherine."

Avery looked up at him. "And then?"

Jakob took a deep breath. "Esteban will sleep on the ship to avoid raising any questions about his activities. But at some point, he will return to that house."

Yes, he would have to.

Avery shuddered at the thought of what he might have done to her.

Jakob pulled his hunting knife and sheath from a cabinet and strapped it to his leg. "When he does, I will be there in your stead."

Bergdis gasped softly and said something to Jakob in Norsk.

Jakob considered his mother and his expression softened. "*Mamma, jeg er en ridder, og det er min plikt å beskytte dronningen og hennes hoff.*" Then he turned to Avery. "I told her that I am a knight, and it is my duty to protect the Queen and her court."

Avery nodded. "God be with you, husband."

§ § §

Jakob was ushered into Catherine's presence immediately. As a knight in her service he deserved that privilege, and as the husband of the queen's dearest friend he always had his sovereign's ear.

Jakob told Catherine what had transpired late that afternoon, explaining why Avery went to visit the ship, and then how Askel was deceived and pulled from his sworn duty.

"But a girl who works the docks, shall we call it, saw Lady Avery being led away by an unsavory man. She followed them, and then came to the Tower to tell me." Jakob laid a hand against his chest. "Unfortunately she was threatened and sent on her way."

Catherine scowled. "So the whore came to tell what she observed, and the guard rebuked her?"

"Yes he did, your Grace."

"How did you come to know about your wife's dangerous circumstance?"

"Lizzy—the whore—waited for anyone she recognized to enter or exit the Tower and carry her message. As fate would have it, I was the first person she came across."

"Thanks to our Father God for that." Catherine crossed herself. "Has the guard been dealt with?"

"Higgins relieved him from the rest of the day's duties, but it is your decision whether additional consequences are due,"

Jakob deferred.

"I shall speak to the king and seek his counsel, but I do believe there must be discipline of some sort. Who can know what other unpleasantness might be averted if handled correctly." Catherine considered Jakob. "What about the whore?"

"When all danger was passed, I rewarded her for her persistence." Jakob flashed a wry smile. "Three pounds sterling."

Catherine huffed. "That was certainly generous, Jakob, considering her situation."

"I owe her everything, your Grace," Jakob softly reminded the queen.

Catherine nodded absently and Jakob thought she was finished with their audience. "What will you do now?"

"With your permission, your Grace," Jakob began. "I shall go find the miscreant, and I shall kill him."

Chapter Ten

Jakob walked back toward the abandoned house and considered his options. First, he could wait outside the house and kill Esteban in the street; but that plan ran the risk of one of the *Albergar's* many drunken sailors noticing and misguidedly coming to Esteban's aid.

The second option was to wait inside the front door. While efficient, Jakob had no desire to sit for the rest of the night in the company of a dead man with half a head.

That left the option of waiting for Esteban in the same room where he imprisoned Avery. While not the quickest path to resolution, at the least Jakob would be able to see the look on Esteban's face when he discovered Jakob in Avery's place.

"This time he will not escape my wrath," Jakob mumbled as he climbed the stairs. "He will receive the very end that he has worked so long and hard to earn."

Jakob closed the door to the room and decided that waiting behind it would give him the best advantage. Once Esteban

opened it and stepped inside the room to search for his prey,
Jakob would push the door closed behind him. After allowing
the Spaniard the briefest moment of recognition and realization,
Jakob's blade would find its home in Esteban's severed heart.

While he waited for the hours to pass, Jakob got up from his
seat on the hearth and paced the length and breadth of the small
room to keep his thigh from stiffening. Though there was no fire
in the fireplace, the room was still less chilled and damp than the
city's smoke-clogged canopy.

He heard the church bells chime the hour. Though the night
would be long, Jakob would not risk missing this encounter.

February 14, 1520

Esteban walked down the *Albergar's* plank an hour before
sunrise. He carried a flask of watered wine and a cloth tied with
hardtack biscuits. While he wanted Avery to be miserable, he
had no desire for her to be dead.

Unless her pompous knight of a husband decided to refute
Esteban's claim, of course. Then the pair of them would deserve
that outcome. And Esteban had no qualms about giving it to
them.

Only after I sample the lady's attributes, of course.

Esteban smiled. He imagined throwing back those expensive
skirts, spreading her unwilling legs, and mounting her with
vigor. He would force her to respond against her will, stroking in
and out relentlessly until she cried out the pleasure she was
unable to deny.

His smile widened.

I believe I will do so no matter how the knight responds.

Esteban adjusted his trousers, his arousal at the punitive idea
confirming the plan.

The house looked the same as it had yester eve, empty and
non-descript. Esteban wrinkled his nose at the memory of the
dead man crumpled on the floor inside the door. He probably
should drag the body to the back of the house so he would not

have to step past it every time he came.

He opened the front door. It scraped across the floor on its sagging hinges and making an annoying sound. Esteban lifted it when he shut it, hoping not to draw any attention from the street. Even though the carousing city was done in for the night, one never knew who might be lurking and looking for trouble.

The man lay where he fell.

Esteban set down the comestibles, grabbed the man by the feet, and dragged him to the back door of the structure. At this point there was no trail of blood to point to the corpse, so he simply shoved the body out the back door and left it as it fell.

"I hope you made your peace, you poor stupid bastard," he mumbled. Then he pulled the door closed and threw the latch.

He returned to the front room and retrieved his supplies. As he climbed the steep stairs, he chuckled.

Time to visit the lady.

§ § §

Jakob heard the front door open. He silently took his position behind the room's solid portal and pressed his ear against it. He heard Esteban grunting and guessed that he was moving the dead man. When the back door below him opened and subsequently closed, Jakob believed that his assumption was correct.

Now Esteban was climbing the stairs.

Jakob drew a slow, bracing breath and pulled the knife from the sheath still strapped to his leg. He grew calm as the years of his knight's training set in. As slow smile lifted his cheeks.

Come and receive your due, you pile of Spanish shit.

The latch wiggled.

"Have you missed me, Avery?" Esteban trilled.

He stepped into the room, now lit by a candle he did not put in place. "What—"

Jakob leaned his bulk against the door, forcing it closed, and shoved Esteban from behind. The former majordomo stumbled forward before he caught himself. He spun to face Jakob, bristling like a homeless cur.

Surprise and fury warred across his dark features. "You!"

Jakob held up his knife. "How dare you try to take *anything* from me?" He kept his tone low and menacing as he stepped forward. "You are nothing. You are no one."

Esteban pulled a knife of his own. "Come and get me, you arrogant ass. I will show you who I am."

Jakob chuckled; a deep, menacing sound.

Esteban's expression shifted briefly, just enough for Jakob to see the man's fear in the candle's light.

"You ask me to *chase* you, little man?" Jakob figured that the Spaniard's pride would be his downfall and chose his taunting words to provoke it. "Because you only attack women and unsuspecting idiots?"

Esteban growled and leapt toward him, knife extended. Jakob twisted to the side and brought his fist down on the back of Esteban's head.

Esteban sprawled flat on his belly, his face hitting the planked floor. When he rolled quickly away from Jakob, blood gushed from his broken nose.

Jakob stepped closer and kicked him in the soft side of his core as hard as his uninjured left leg allowed. "Stand up!"

Esteban rolled again. This time he hit the wall.

"I said stand up!" Jakob bellowed his anger. "Or do you choose to die like the dog you are?"

Esteban used the wall to help him clamber to his feet. He hesitated just a moment, then screamed and launched himself at Jakob.

The knight was ready.

Jakob deflected the blade with one arm while he used the force of Esteban's hurtling body to drive his own blade deep into the Spaniard's chest. He felt the jarring rasp of bone as it slid between Esteban's ribs.

Esteban gasped.

Blood gushed over Jakob's hand, still gripping the knife.

Esteban dropped his knife. He glared at Jakob with a stunned yet livid gaze.

"Damn you to hell," he whispered.

"Wait for me there," Jakob growled. He yanked his knife from the other man's chest and stepped back.

Esteban dropped to his knees, his life's blood spurting from the gash in his shirt.

Jakob leaned down and murmured in his ear, "I must warn you. It will be a *very* long wait."

With a moaning groan Esteban slid sideways and sprawled senseless on the floor.

Jakob wiped the blood from his knife on Esteban's trousers before sliding it back into its sheath. Then he pulled a crucifix from his tunic, kissed it, and crossed himself.

Forgive me Father, for I have sinned.

§ § §

"Is he dead?" Lizzy asked. The whore had sidled up to Jakob the minute he stepped into the pre-dawn street.

"Yes." Jakob looked down at the girl. "Do you sleep?"

"I'll go now. But I wanted to make sure."

Jakob nodded. "Go. It is done, and all are safe."

Lizzy grabbed his still-bloody hand and kissed it. "God bless ye, Sir."

Then she disappeared into the fog.

Jakob limped up Tower Hill; in spite of his best efforts, the damp cold and forced inactivity over the last several hours conspired to stiffen his right thigh. His next task was to assign a group of servants to retrieve the two dead men from the abandoned house and bring their bodies to the fortress.

After that, he would summon Captain Moreno from the *Albergar* and have him identify Esteban. Jakob would ask the captain to tell him everything he knew about the dead sailor.

Hopefully all of Jakob's questions would be answered in the process.

"He had better bring the ledgers," Jakob added to the message he was sending a squire to deliver. "And he'll want to thoroughly examine the man's room to see what he might have stolen."

"Yes, Sir."

Jakob looked at the young man who reminded him of himself over a decade earlier. "Have you got all of that?"

The squire repeated the message perfectly.

"Good. And do not come back without Moreno," Jakob charged him. "Even if you have to sit on his desk until he agrees."

The squire grinned. "I understand, Sir. I shall return with the Captain in tow."

Jakob turned toward his house. He planned to ask Askel for a hot bath in which to soak his leg later, and while he waited for the captain he would hold his wife in his arms.

No one will ever take her from me.

No one.

Chapter Eleven

February 21, 1520

Avery sat in a carriage on the pier, sheltered from the rain, and watched the *Albergar* slowly move down the Thames on the outgoing tide. The trade ship was making her way back to Spain loaded with Norse and English goods and Avery stood to make a substantial profit.

The ten days which her ship spent in London's port brought both joy in the unexpected arrival of Jakob's mother Bergdis, and distress as Esteban Gonzales sought personal revenge for being caught embezzling from his dead employer, Avery's first husband.

Now she was glad to see the ship sail once more, hoping and praying that the troubles the debauched Paolo Mendoza left behind were finally put down.

Jakob proved right in his assumption that Esteban was the ship's purser. Captain Moreno responded to the summons to identify his dead crewman, and that same day one body was buried and the other burned.

"It will be the beginning of his eternity in flames," Jakob muttered as they watched the pyre. "And now we are truly done with him."

Once the situation was fully explained—and that Gonzalo Esteban was in truth Esteban Gonzales, Avery's former majordomo—Captain Moreno himself searched every nook of Esteban's cabin.

"Nearly nine hundred pounds," he told Avery later as he handed Jakob a weighty bag of gold and silver coins. "I am sorry that I cannot say which transactions were logged incorrectly to hide the theft."

Avery assured him that did not matter at the moment. "What does matter is that the money is returned to me and will help to replay my debt to Queen Catherine."

Captain Moreno gave her a quirky smile. "I have never worked for a woman before, Lady Avery, but I have been impressed by your keen mind for business."

She felt her cheeks warming. "Thank you, Captain. That means quite a lot to me. I shall write to Gustavo Salazar and commend you to him for your loyal service."

The captain bowed. "Thank you, my lady."

Avery knocked on the roof of the carriage. It was time to go back home. Preparations for King Henry's lavish Valentine's Ball celebrating Percival Bethington's astonishing nuptials were frantically being completed.

"Four days, Percy," Avery mused. "And you will be a married man."

February 23, 1520

"We cannot find Bethington."

Avery paused as Emily was dressing her for dinner and turned wide eyes to Jakob. "What do you mean 'cannot find'?"

Jakob scuttled his fingers through his hair. "He was supposed to attend a final fitting for his costume, but he did not appear as scheduled."

"His costume for the ball, is that correct?" Her brows pulled together over her dark eyes. On most women this expression was unattractive, but on his beautiful wife it was a signal that her keen mind was whirring.

"Yes. He is wearing his Golden Fleece attire for the church ceremony."

"Could it be that he simply forgot?"

Jakob shook his head. "You know how much he relishes these sorts of occasions."

"Yes, but…" Avery raised a single finger in denial. "That was when he was unencumbered and had his pick of women for the evening's entertainment."

"And now that he is about to be married, he spurns the idea?" That could sound like Bethington.

Except it did not.

"Percy has nothing but glowing words for his betrothed," Jakob stated. "So much so, that I find myself awash in bad poetic comparisons whenever he speaks of her."

Avery told Emily to finish dressing her. "Let us wait and see if he attends supper. Perhaps there is nothing to be concerned about."

§ § §

Avery watched Anne Woodcote carefully. The daughter of Lord Basil Woodcote, Earl of Oxford, was only nineteen but possessed the self-assure mien of a much older woman. Her blonde curls brushed over her shoulder and her pale blue eyes attended to her dinner companions.

None of which were Percy.

Avery noticed a slight but distinct decrease in the girl's normally effusive composure and though attentive, her eyes were not smiling. Anne knew something was amiss. Whether she knew *why* it was amiss was a different question.

Jakob settled into the chair beside Avery.

"Have you had any luck?" she asked softly.

"He is not inside the Tower grounds as best I can tell." Jakob claimed his stein of ale and took a sizeable gulp. "I shall begin a search of taverns after I have eaten."

"I do hope he has not done anything foolish." Avery glanced at Percival's petite fiancée. "She truly does love him."

Jakob motioned for a servant to refill his ale. "And if he is foolish enough to throw her over—and his child—then I will personally beat him to a bloody pulp."

§ § §

Bergdis Hansen thanked Emily for her supper tray. And she did it in English.

The maid smiled at her. "You are welcome, my lady. Do you wish for anything else?"

Bergdis understood the reply *you are welcome* and assumed the question was the same one as every time. "No. Thank you. *Dette er bra.*"

"All is braw then. Good."

Bergdis nodded. "*Ja. God.*"

Emily curtsied and went back toward the kitchen, presumably for her own meal.

Some Norsk words such as *bra* and *god* sounded like their English counterparts and that made things easier. Other words had nothing in common, however, and Bergdis wondered—if she decided to remain in England—would she master the new language before she died.

"It is good for the mind," she reminded herself as she dipped her spoon into the bowl of steaming savory stew. "An idle mind gives up. Besides, I am not that old. I have time."

Bergdis stared into the cheerful fire as she enjoyed her well-made but solitary meal. Jakob always insisted that she was welcome to attend dinner with the court but she found the boisterous crowd, all babbling too rapidly for her to attempt to follow, uninviting and intimidating.

"I am a simple woman from a village in a small country," she told her son. "I am more comfortable on my own."

"Are you certain?" Avery asked her in her oddly-accented Norsk. "We are happy and you are with us."

"Yes. Thank you, Daughter." Bergdis squeezed Avery's hand. "Do not worry over me."

Bergdis broke a piece of bread and dipped it in the stew. The cook Jakob employed was from Denmark and she understood the sort of flavors that Bergdis was accustomed to. By the same token, the woman was introducing her to English fare, easing her way by starting with dishes that were similar to Norwegian food.

All in all, Bergdis was very satisfied that she had drummed up enough courage to step on Avery's ship and make this journey to London. Of course Johan had tried to talk her out of it, but every argument he presented only made her more determined.

"I am neither too old nor too incapable of managing my affairs," she stated. "And I will be sailing on my daughter-in-law's ship. My welfare will be seen to."

"But how will you communicate, Mamma?" he pressed.

Several months ago Bergdis had a conversation about languages with Jakob, after he appeared so unexpectedly at Hansen Hall in Arendal with his Spanish wife in tow. So she knew that answer.

"I will listen for words that sound like Norsk or Latin. And I will use my hands to gesture."

And she had.

Thinking about the ship now brought back a surge of the bone-deep fear which she experienced several days ago when that ship's purser abducted Avery.

Bergdis had never seen her son so cold and determined as she had the night he strapped the dirk to his leg. His words, *I am a knight, and it is my duty to protect the Queen and her court* thrummed through her core as he spoke them, and she suddenly saw him as the man he was, not the boy she knew so many years ago.

Jakob had grown up. He had become a member of two royal courts, trusted by both of the sovereigns he had served to do their highest bidding. On the one hand, he moved with intelligent grace and wisdom through the intricacies of court politics, a true gentleman in every sense of the word.

Yet on the other hand, when required to do so, he used his considerable strength and skill to dispatch anyone who posed a threat to those whom he served and loved. And he did not flinch in that duty. Not for a moment.

For the hundredth time, Bergdis wished Fafnir could have seen the man his second son had become. If her husband had not been so stubborn, Jakob would not have been estranged from the family for so many years.

But if Jakob had not inherited that same stubborn streak, he would not have left Arendal to follow his own path.

Bergdis sipped her wine, smiling into her glass at that thought.

All has come right in the end, I suppose.

A sudden pounding on the door summoned Askel from the kitchen. Emily followed, her eyes wide with concern.

"Stay where you are, Lady Hansen," Askel said in Norsk. "I shall see who has come."

Emily picked up Bergdis' supper tray and hurried back into the kitchen. Bergdis straightened in her chair and smoothed her hair and skirts.

Another round of fists on the door made her uneasy.

Askel gripped the latch and lifted it. With a steadying breath he opened the door.

"Sir Bethington?" The valet's tone reflected his surprise. "Sir Hansen is at supper in the Tower."

"I know." The beefy knight stepped inside. His face was ruddier than usual and Bergdis could smell beer from her seat. "I have not come to speak with Jakob."

A confused Askel moved out of the man's way. "What do you wish, Sir?"

Percival Bethington's gaze rested on Bergdis. "I have come to speak with his mother."

Chapter Twelve

After a hurried supper, Jakob kissed his wife on the cheek and left the Tower grounds to search surrounding taverns for the elusive Percy. He had no idea what might have pulled his English counterpart from the side of his beloved betrothed only days before their wedding, but he was determined to find out.

Percy had several favorite spots near the fortress, chosen for their level of cleanliness and the quality of their food. Jakob worked his way through the establishments in a methodical manner, speaking to the barkeeps at each one.

After all, they did know Bethington well.

"Nah, I ain't seen him today," said the burly owner of The White Crow. "Is there trouble?"

"I am not certain," Jakob admitted. "He seems to have gone missing."

The man snorted. "He's about t' be married, ain't he?"

"Yes."

"Check the whorehouses is my advice."

Lizzy.

Jakob wondered if there was a way to track the girl down. While she seemed to have an uncanny penchant for showing up at just the right time, he had no idea where she went afterwards.

Jakob had two more taverns to visit.

Then I shall go looking for her.

§ § §

Bergdis recoiled in surprise. She recognized the words *come*, *speak*, and *mother*. Had the English knight truly come to see her?

Askel stared at Bethington. "She does not speak English."

"*Jeg snakker litt Norsk,*" he replied, his eyes still on Bergdis.

"Come." She waved toward the big chair nearest hers. "Sit."

"Thank you. *Takk du.*" Percival crossed the room hesitantly. He lowered himself into the upholstered seat.

"*Vil du ha en drink?*" Bergdis asked if he wanted a drink.

"*Ja. Takk.*"

Askel lifted the decanter of wine and poured the Englishman a glass. "Can I get you anything else?"

Percival shook his head. "No."

"Do you want me to stay and translate?" he asked, then asked again in Norsk for Bergdis' sake. "*Vil du at jeg skal bo og oversette?*"

Bergdis watched Percival carefully. She sensed that whatever he wanted to discuss needed to be spoken of privately.

"No," she said to Askel. "He and I talk."

Percy sighed his relief. "Yes. Thank you."

Askel walked to the door leading to the kitchen. "Summon me if you need help."

Bergdis nodded. Then she faced the distraught knight and asked what was wrong. "*Hva er galt?*"

Percy looked like he might cry. "I am terrified."

"Terrified?" she repeated with a frown.

Percival nodded. "I have great *frykt.*"

"*Hvorfor? Fordi du skal gifte?*" Bergdis asked, but did not believe this was the reason.

"No, I am not afraid of marrying." His expression eased. "Anne is the best thing that has happened in my life. I do not want to live without her."

The only word Bergdis understood for certain was *no*. "Then *hvorfor*, Percival?"

He rubbed his hands over his ruddy cheeks. "I am afraid of becoming a father."

§ § §

Jakob exhausted all of Bethington's regular haunts without finding a trace of the Englishman. If Percival was not as imposing a figure as he was and well skilled in the arts of battle, Jakob might fear that the knight had encountered an unfortunate circumstance.

"No, he is just being obstinate," Jakob muttered into the night. His breath formed a cloud of fog in front of his face.

The time had come to search out Lizzy.

Jakob walked the mile back to Tower Hill. Between that grassy rise and the docks he expected he would find the girl plying her trade. What he did not expect was how she looked when he did come across her.

"Lizzy?" Jakob approached the whore. "Is that a new dress?"

She giggled and spun in a slow circle. "Aye. Thanks to your generosity."

"You look quite pretty." Jakob tried to keep the surprise out of his tone, but it was a struggle.

"Ye have changed my life, Sir." Her earnest gaze struck his heart. "I've moved to a better place of business. And because it's cleaner, and my dress is new, I can charge more for my services."

"I am glad to hear that," was his awkward response. Could he be glad she was still whoring? But then, an uneducated single girl in London had scant other options.

"I plan to save enough to buy my own place," she continued, her excitement clear. "Might be I get another girl or two to work with me."

"Miss Lizzy the brothel owner?" Jakob chuckled. "Who might have expected that?"

"Not me. Not before." Her smile turned wistful. "But ye and Lady Avery have been kind."

"I am glad we could help you." He truly was.

Lizzy reached out and tapped a finger on his arm. "Ye know, brothels are good investments. No matter what else happens in the world, men want their pleasures."

Jakob did laugh at that. "I shall discuss the idea with my wife."

Lizzy bounced a grinning nod. "Ye do that."

Jakob's smile faded. "Now I need your help, Lizzy. Have you seen Sir Bethington anywhere this night?"

§ § §

"I find I am overwhelmed by the prospect." Percival stood and began to pace the length of the drawing room. "How can I, a man with such a storied reputation, ever hope to be a suitable father to an impressionable boy?"

"*Ingen vet hvordan å være en far før han er en.*"

Bergdis did not understand his words any more than she believed he understood hers. But that did not matter. What did matter was that the knight felt free to express his thoughts, and that her tone was soothing and reassuring in response.

"No one?" He squinted at her. "Is this true?"

"Yes." Bergdis smiled softly, pleased that he grasped her main point. "*Du vil bli en god far, fordi du ønsker å være.*"

Percival looked askance at her. "I will be a good father?"

"Yes." Bergdis nodded. "You want this."

He shook his head. "Just because I want to bring the boy up in the manner in which I should, does not mean I will not fail…"

In the face of his obvious deflection Bergdis decided to change course. "And the mother?"

His shoulders drooped. "Anne will be perfect. She already is perfect. She will put me to shame."

There was something good and something bad in those

words. Bergdis took a risk and responded to what she assumed he said. "Mother is good. And then you are good."

Percival reclaimed his chair. "Are you saying that I will be a good father to my son, because Anne will be a good mother?" his brow eased. "I will learn from watching her?"

Bergdis nodded. Whatever the knight heard was what he wanted to hear. Or needed to hear. There was just one more thing.

"*Hvis du har en datter, vil du være en god far for henne også.*"

Percival's face went white as Bergdis' linen napkin. "A daughter?"

§ § §

Lizzy walked a few yards in front of Jakob so as not to gain unwanted attention. She stopped acquaintances she knew and slipped into taverns and inns where she trusted the owners, to enquire about the big English knight.

Using the information she gleaned, they followed a crooked path through an area of London which Jakob was only slightly familiar with, and only then because of his many carriage rides when he played the part of the king.

Thank God that is finished.

"He was here most recently," Lizzy said after exiting an inn. She turned back and began to walk in the direction from which they had come. "The girl followed him a ways, hoping to get him to bed her, but he said no. Said he was going home."

"Back to the Tower?" Jakob shook his head. "Percy you will drive me insane, I swear it is true."

"Shall I walk back with ye, Sir?"

Jakob looked down at the girl. "No, but thank you. Your help has been immeasurable." He reached into his pocket and fished for coins.

Lizzy put up a hand. "Ye don't owe me anything."

Jakob stopped walking and grabbed her hand. He pressed the two silver coins into her palm and closed her fingers around them. "Consider this my first investment."

Lizzy's eyes teared, the moisture sparkling in the lamplight. "You are a good man, Sir Hansen. I will remember ye in my prayers."

The prayers of a whore?

Jesus Himself walked with the worst of the worst.

"Thank you, Lizzy. Lady Avery and I appreciate that."

§ § §

"Daughter is good. Loves a father. *Alltid.*"

Percival looked as if he had been punched in the chest. "I will need to protect her from men like me."

Bergdis leaned forward and gripped his big beefy hands in her aged ones. The contrast was startling to her, but it made what she wanted to say that much more poignant.

"Percival Bethington, *du har et godt hjerte. Med bønn og veiledning, kan du ikke mislykkes. Dine barn vil stå frem og velsigne deg. Jeg lover deg.*"

"Thank you, Lady Hansen." He leaned forward and kissed her cheek. "If my mother herself were here, she could not have set me right with more skillfulness."

§ § §

Jakob threw the front door to his house wide open with irritated force. He froze when he faced Bergdis holding Percival's hands, the pair sitting cozily together in his drawing room. The English knight's cheeks were damp and he hurriedly wiped them dry.

"Bethington! I have been out these past hours searching the city for you!" Jakob shut the door hard behind him. "What were you about, man?"

Percival stood. "I apologize, Jakob. I did not mean to be gone so long."

Jakob crossed the room. "Why were you gone in the first place?"

"Jakob…" His mother's voice held a warning tone that sent him straight back to his childhood.

He clamped his jaw shut, lest he snap at her like a petulant adolescent.

"I was experiencing a sense of distress, Jakob," Percy began. "It overwhelmed me."

"Distress over your marriage?" Jakob assumed.

"No." Percy shook his head. "Distress over my impending fatherhood."

Jakob relaxed a little. He walked to the sideboard and poured himself a cup of wine. In spite of all the taverns and inns he had visited this evening, he never remained in any establishment long enough to purchase refreshment.

"You had us worried," he grumbled when he faced Bethington again. "Do not do this again."

"I will not." A small smile lifted the knight's cheeks. "I am recovered."

Jakob saw the satisfied look on Bergdis' face. "Did my mother have a hand in your restoration?"

Bethington nodded and smiled fully at the seated woman. "She is the reason I am restored."

Askel entered the room. "I came inside and heard your voice. Is there anything you need, Sir?"

Jakob used his wine glass to indicate the unlikely pair. "Can you explain what went on here?"

Askel nodded. "Sir Bethington came to speak with your mother."

"Did you translate?"

"No."

Jakob returned his attention to Percival, his brows pulling together. "What did she say to you?"

"I gave no idea." Percival laughed. "But she said it with consummate wisdom and absolute perfection."

Chapter Twelve

February 25, 1520

Avery and Jakob, with Bergdis on his arm, escaped the sleet slicing nearly sideways across London and entered the shelter of Westminster Abbey a quarter of an hour before the noon mass. Percival Bethington was in seated in the front row of the benches between the choir and the altar. Jakob and Avery joined him as other court members trickled in and filled the space behind them.

In stark contrast to a few nights ago, Percival appeared completely calm. Dressed in his Golden Fleece finery he cut a stunning figure, as did Jakob. Those members of the Tudor court who had not seen the knights dressed thusly kept casting surreptitious gazes in their direction.

Avery smiled.

My husband is the handsomer of the two.

"I think this also," Bergdis whispered to Avery.

Avery turned to her mother-in-law. "Are you a mind reader?"

Bergdis chuckled. "My son has beauty. Yes?"

"Yes." Avery leaned closer and whispered, "He got it from his mother."

Anne Woodcote entered Westminster Abbey with her father and mother and walked purposefully to the front of the church.

"Good day, Sir Bethington," she said when she reached Percival's side. "It is a splendid day for a wedding, do you not agree?"

Percival stood and bowed to his fiancée. "This is indeed a remarkably fine day."

Anne turned a radiant smile to Avery. "Do you not agree, Lady Avery?"

Avery's toes were chilled to numbness because the sleet has soaked through her slippers. Even so, she grinned at the young bride.

"It could not be more perfect, Lady Anne."

Wedding masses were the same as regular masses but with the added sacrament of marriage added in. As the congregation waded patiently through the liturgical morass, Avery noticed that Percival was having trouble sitting still.

"Nervous, my lord?" she teased.

Percy beamed at her. "Eager, my lady."

When the moment for the marriage sacrament arrived, Percival stood and stepped into the aisle. He extended his left elbow. Anne stood as well and tucked her arm in his. The couple walked forward together.

Jakob followed and stood behind Percy on his right.

As their promises were made and their vows spoken, Avery grew teary-eyed. This was the first wedding she had attended since her own and it prompted a rush of intense emotion. The extreme measures she went to on that one fateful day which secured her future a year ago, also secured her marriage.

Thank You, Father. I am richly blessed.

Bergdis took hold of her hand and Avery turned toward her mother in law. "I am happy and you husband Jakob."

Avery smiled at the broken English, warmed to her core by the sentiment. "I am happy, too."

"Amen."

Avery returned her attention to the priest. The trio in front of her all kneeled in preparation for the sacrament of communion. Avery had a moment of concern for Jakob's leg, coming in from the cold damp day into the equally cold cathedral and kneeling on stones that never warmed up. But when it came time for them to stand he did not seem affected.

The mass ended, nearly an hour after it began, with the pronouncement that Anne Woodcote and Percival Bethington were now husband and wife and that no man could put that bond asunder.

Jakob returned to her side as the newly wedded couple made their way to the back of the church.

"It is finished." Jakob flashed a lop-sided grin as he parroted Jesus' last words on the cross. "I wish him at least half of the happiness I have found with you."

Avery tucked herself under her tall husband's arm. "And I wish them the same."

Jakob offered his free arm to his mother. "Now we have the wedding luncheon, and then we prepare for the Valentine's Ball."

Avery laughed. "Are you ready?"

"As ever I shall be," Jakob groaned.

§ § §

Henry the Eighth was well known for his lavish parties, usually accompanied by performances of his original songs and poetry, and often involving some sort of trick.

The last trick Jakob experienced was when Henry and he dressed identically and Jakob was instructed to pretend to be the king whenever he was approached. That was the night Avery discovered Jakob's deal with the human devil that Henry so often proved to be.

Jakob did not expect any sort of similar trickery tonight since his choice of costume was his alone. He opted for a simple red velvet tunic which he could easily wear again, serviceable gray hose, and tall black boots. As a nod to the theme, his pleated-sleeved shirt flashed glimpses of red inside the pleats—secret love, as he called it—and he wore a half-mask in the shape of an upside-down heart.

Avery did not let him see her costume and was dressing in Catherine's chamber tonight. All she would tell him was that it was Catherine's suggestion, and the queen had a heavy hand in its design.

"I hope you find it as clever as Catherine does," Avery told him as she was preparing to join the queen after the wedding luncheon. "And even if you don't, please lie to her."

Jakob had to admit his curiosity was piqued.

Bergdis was invited to the Ball along with him and Avery and, to Jakob's great surprise, she accepted.

"I want to experience this extravagant evening," she told her son. "When else will I have this chance?"

Four or five times a year, if you remain with us.

"Then you must enjoy yourself, Mamma." Jakob kissed his mother's forehead. "You deserve every frivolous bit of enjoyment which comes your way."

When Bergdis declared herself dressed and coifed as finely as she could be, Jakob escorted her to the Tower and the ballroom. At one end of the large space was a tiered balcony where attendees were able to escape the crush of the crowd and still keep an eye on the festivities. That was where Jakob safely deposited his mother.

"I shall attend to you regularly, Mamma," he promised. "When you wish to return home, simply wave and I will fetch you."

"Thank you." Bergdis' gaze was moving over the gathering revelers, all in colorful costume. "This spectacle is breathtaking, Jakob. I could not imagine such a display."

He smiled. It was true that words failed in the description of the pageantry that defined King Henry's lifestyle. "Would you care for refreshment, Mamma?"

Bergdis shook her head. "Not as yet."

Jakob waved a hand toward the back of the balcony.

"Servants will come up here periodically, so feel free to ask for anything you desire."

"Thank you, Jakob."

Jakob kissed his mother's hand and made his way back down to the floor, wondering as he did when Queen Catherine would make her appearance and he could finally see what sort of costume she had cooked up for her chief lady-in-waiting.

§ § §

Anne Woodcote could only be described as radiant perfection. Her dusky pink silk gown complemented her coloring perfectly. Percival Bethington was a very lucky man.

"Lady Anne, you look stunning," Avery effused as they waited for Catherine to enter the ballroom. "And congratulations on your marriage. Your husband is a man of exceptional character."

Anne laughed in a pretty, musical trill. "If by your words you mean that he *is* a character, you are quite correct, Lady Avery." Her expression softened and she continued, "But he is *my* character at last."

The Queen appeared in the startling gown she chose intentionally to declare her particular situation. Avery tried to gently suggest that provoking the king might not be the best plan, but Catherine was adamant.

"I want Henry to both understand my pain, and realize that he is the cause of it."

Catherine paused in the private hallway leading into the public space and her costumed court gathered behind her. She nodded at the servants standing beside the doors, ready to pull them open and admit their sovereign into the ballroom.

"Let us join the festivities."

The doors opened and Catherine swept into the ball, head held high. A hushed gasp slithered through the crowd.

Catherine's beautifully tailored and embellished gown was made entirely of black, from the ruffled silk underskirts, to the black-on-black pattern of the brocade, and to the black lace at her throat and wrists.

She even borrowed Avery's black Spanish lace fan.

The stunning expanse of fitted black elegance was only broken by a scarlet sash. Pleated and pinned to Catherine's left shoulder, the fabric opened as it crossed her torso and rested in its full breadth on her right hip.

"It represents my wounded heart," she explained to Avery when she designed it. "And the depths of my despair.

The last part of her display was her intricate lace mask— solid black with a red ruby teardrop below each eyehole.

Henry, who was already in the ballroom, glared angrily at his queen. His costume, by shocking contrast, was that of Cupid, the Roman god of love, complete with feathered wings and bow.

Avery watched Henry, wondering if he would make a larger ruckus than Catherine had by her choice of apparel. Judging by the quiet crowd everyone in attendance was wondering the same thing.

Henry drew a deep breath, forced a strained smile, and bowed to Catherine. When he straightened, she gave him a polite curtsy.

He walked toward her with his back stiff and his chin high. He took her hand, held it above her head, and addressed the crowd.

"While I have chosen to embrace romantic love on this occasion, as we celebrate the happy marriage of Sir Percival Bethington to the beautiful Lady Anne Woodcote, my wife has chosen a different path. Please do not allow her appearance to dampen your mood."

Avery sucked her breath and held it. Henry's public chastisement of Catherine was unexpected and unprecedented and she wondered if her friend would turn tail and run in the face of it.

For a moment, no one moved.

Then the Queen smiled at her king. In contrast to her husband's, Catherine's smile was not in the least bit strained.

"Why would my depiction of the vibrant passions of love in the darkness of a beautiful night dampen anyone's mood?" she challenged.

Avery gasped again. Catherine obviously expected Henry to say something unpleasant to her about her costume and had conjured her rebuttal in advance.

Snickers of appreciation scattered around the room.

"I will drink to that!" someone called out. Avery hoped Henry did not recognize the voice, or the man would be permanently banished before sunrise.

Henry's eyes narrowed. "How could I have mistaken such an obvious purpose, as I am so well acquainted with the passions of the night."

Catherine's cheeks flushed violently and Avery could only imagine the retorts Catherine could throw at the king.

Please, my friend, keep your head.

The Queen dipped her chin. "Yes, dear husband. As my many confinements have irrefutably proven."

As the jabs went back and forth between them, Avery felt like she was watching one of Henry's tennis matches. Only this time, the king was most definitely bested.

Catherine grinned happily and addressed the revelers before Henry could utter another word. "Let us all toast to the love and passion of our celebrated newlyweds!"

Chapter Thirteen

Jakob made his way toward his wife, stunned by the exchange that had just taken place. On this night he was again relieved that he served Queen Catherine and not the volatile Henry.

When he reached her, Jakob took Avery's elbow. She turned around to face him, her expression displaying her shock.

"I do not know what to say..." she murmured.

Jakob pulled her away from Catherine. "Would you like something to eat?" he asked loud enough to be heard by anyone nearby who might be listening.

Avery was quiet as he escorted her to a table laden with every variety of meats and cheeses that Jakob could think of. "Tell me about your very interesting costume."

Avery coughed a laugh, clearly relieved to change the subject of their conversation. "I am a ship."

Jakob stepped back and took a careful look. "Explain, please."

"These wide pleats…" Avery ran her hands along the broad folds of brown watered silk which curved outward from a central point at her waist and continued around to the back of her wide skirt. "Are the boards which make up the ship."

Jakob chuckled. "Yes. I can see that now."

"My bodice is intended to mimic the apparel of a ship's captain." Avery held out her arms; white linen drooped in billowy folds that were gathered at her wrists. "And my sleeves, of course, are the sails."

Jakob began filling their plates. "And how does this represent love?"

"Sailing the seas of love, or some such sentiment."

Avery turned around. On the back of her bodice was a red heart outlined in seed pearls. She looked back at him over her shoulder and grinned.

"The heart was an afterthought. Catherine was so enamored of the idea of dressing me like one of my ships, she forgot the overall theme."

"Hansen!"

Jakob turned toward the familiar and robust voice. "Bethington—too late to back out now, my friend."

The big knights clasped each other's forearms and shook them affectionately.

"I shall never," Percival said, crossing his heart with his free hand. "I become more convinced by the minute that I am happily caught and tamed."

"And I could not be happier for you."

Percival turned to Avery. "And thank you, dear lady, for spurning my advances so incontestably."

Avery laughed. "That is quite an odd thing to thank someone for—but you are very welcome, Sir."

Percival wagged a finger at her. "Think about it. If you had succumbed to my substantial wit and charm, you would not have this hulking Nordic beast as your husband now."

Avery smiled up at Jakob. "You do speak the truth, Percy."

Anne approached the trio and Percival pulled his new wife close to his side, looping his muscled arm around her narrow shoulders. "And I would never have been caught by this conniving witch of a girl."

Bethington's delirious grin belied his teasing words. "And my impending fatherhood would not be such a joyous end."

"We are truly happy for both of you," Avery cooed.

Bethington startled, a sudden thought claiming his attention. "Anne, would you be averse to having Jakob and Avery as little Percival's godparents?"

Anne blinked as the sudden shift caught her off guard, then she smiled at her husband. "I could not imagine anyone better."

§ § §

Avery suggested to Jakob that they use his mother as an excuse to leave the ball earlier than they normally would, and was glad when he agreed.

"God parents," Jakob said as they walked across the Tower grounds. "That was an unexpected subject for the occasion."

"I never imagined that Percival Bethington would be a father, much less that I would be someone's god father," Jakob continued.

Avery smiled in the dim light. "I agree with the first half of your statement, Jakob, but I believe that the second half was inevitable once the deed was done."

"What do you mean?" he asked.

"Think about it for a minute." Avery stopped walking and faced her husband. "Anne Woodcote planned to marry Percy years ago. Not one occurrence since then has been accidental."

Jakob translated the story to his mother and asked, "What has that to do with god parents?"

"I am Queen Catherine's chief lady-in-waiting and her dearest friend. You are a knight in the Queen's service who has connections to King Henry. If anything happens to Anne or Percy, their child will remain in the protection of the royal court."

Jakob chuckled as he explained this to his mother.

"Your wife has very good..." Bergdis tapped the side of her

head. "*Tenker.*"

Thinking. Avery squeezed her hand. "Thank you, Bergdis."

Avery resumed their walk across the grounds of the Tower. "If Anne was not such a delight, I might fault her for conniving. As it is, I look forward to her companionship for years to come."

Jakob opened their front door and they stepped inside the cozy warmth of the house. When neither Askel nor Emily appeared to assist them, Jakob called out Askel's name.

"Coming, Sir."

The valet crossed from the kitchen through the dining room and into the drawing room. He was sporting a massive bruise on his cheek and that eye was swollen nearly shut. Emily scurried behind him, a wet cloth in her hand.

"What happened to you?" Avery blurted.

"It is nothing, my lady." Askel held out hand with bloodied knuckles. "Let me help you."

"Not with those hands!" Avery shrugged her cloak off and helped Bergdis out of hers. She draped the discarded outerwear over the nearest chair.

Jakob did the same, demanding that Askel explain his injuries. "Now."

"It is my fault, Sir." Emily had clearly been crying. "He got in a fight because of me."

"Not you," Askel snapped. "Denys."

"Bethington's valet?" Jakob shot a confused glance toward Avery. "I believed you two were friends."

"We were—we are." Askel shrugged. "I hope."

Emily stepped forward. "Denys asked me to marry him."

"When?" Jakob asked.

"This evening." Emily looked sideways at Askel. "He came here during the ball."

"He tried to snatch her out from under me," Askel growled. Avery noticed how much improved his English was of a sudden and she bit back a smile.

The result of true love with an English maid?

Emily spun to face him. "He could not have if you had ever, even just once, spoken your mind."

"I planned to."

Emily stomped a foot. "Well, planning is not doing, is it then?"

Askel looked sufficiently cowed. "No."

Jakob stepped bravely into the breach. "If I understand, Askel, you had a romantic interest in Emily but neglected to tell her."

He nodded.

"And Emily, had he expressed his interest, you would have been amenable?"

She scowled at the valet. "Yes. Of course."

"Then this evening, Denys came calling and made a proposal of his own…" Jakob continued.

"Not one I had ever encouraged, Sir," Emily stated. "Not enthusiastically, anyway."

Avery smothered another smile. "But when he did so, then Askel objected. Enthusiastically."

Jakob rested his hands on his hips and addressed Askel. "How bad does Denys look?"

He shrugged. "About the same as me, I guess."

Emily folded her arms. "I stepped between them before they killed each other."

"That was good thinking." Jakob considered the maid. "How does the situation stand now?"

Her expression softened and she glanced at Askel. "I would *like* to be a married woman."

Askel straightened and pinned her with his good eye. "Would you consent to marry me, then?"

"Are you asking me?"

The valet wisely dropped to one knee. "With all my heart."

Emily smiled for the first time that night, a bright happy smile that stretched her cheeks farther than Avery had ever seen them.

"Yes, Askel. I will marry you."

Chapter Fourteen

July 29, 1520

Jakob and Avery stood alongside Percival and Anne in King Henry's newly rebuilt Chapel Royal of Saint Peter ad Vincula. The resident priest was preparing to perform the first infant baptism held in the Tower's little refurbished church.

Anne cradled her daughter in her arms while Percy looked ready to burst with pride.

"He's a girl," he told Jakob as they celebrated at one of Bethington's favorite pubs. "And he's the prettiest thing I have ever seen."

Jakob laughed at Percy's choice of words. "The next one will be a boy, certainly."

"I cannot care." Percy lifted his filled stein. "She has claimed my heart."

The priest stopped his fussing preparations and faced the two couples. "Are we ready?"

Percival grinned. "Yes, Father."

The middle-aged man began with reading a scripture in Latin, and then bowed his head in prayer.

When he finished, Anne handed the blanketed bundle to the priest. He spoke words of blessing over the babe and anointed her head with oil.

Then he handed the child to Jakob while he addressed both couples. "Do you each promise to raise this child in the one and only Catholic Church, and to bring her up in the knowledge of the one true God?"

"We do," they said in unison.

He nodded. "How shall she be called?"

Percy answered, "Priscilla Anne Bethington."

The priest wet his fingers and sprinkled holy water on the girls' forehead. "I baptize thee Priscilla Anne Bethington in the Name of the Father, and the Son, and the Holy Ghost. Amen."

Another anointing with oil, another Latin prayer, and a few final words of blessing concluded the private ceremony.

As the couples emerged on this humid summer day the stench of the Tower moat assaulted them.

"Somebody needs to drain that thing," Jakob grumbled.

Avery laughed and looped her arm through her husband's as they followed Percy and Anne toward the couple's new home inside the Tower walls.

"Never mind that. I am famished."

Jakob smiled and contently kissed the top of her head.

THE HANSEN FAMILY TREE

Sveyn Hansen* (b. 1035 ~ Arendal, Norway)

***

Rydar Hansen (b. 1324 ~ Arendal, Norway)
Grier MacInnes (b. 1328 ~ Durness, Scotland)

Eryndal Bell Hansen (b. 1327 ~ Bedford, England)
Andrew Drummond (b. 1325 ~ Falkirk, Scotland)

***

Jakob Petter Hansen (b. 1485 ~ Arendal, Norway)
Avery Galaviz de Mendoza (b. 1483 ~ Madrid, Spain)

***

Brander Hansen (b. 1689 ~ Arendal, Norway)
Regin Kildahl (b. 1693 ~ Hamar, Norway)

***

Martin Hansen (b. 1721 ~ Arendal, Norway)
Dagne Sivertsen (b. 1725 ~ Ljan, Norway)

Reidar Hansen (b. 1750 ~ Boston, Massachusetts)
Kristen Sven (b. 1754 ~ Philadelphia, Pennsylvania)

Nicolas Hansen (b. 1787 ~ Cheltenham, Missouri Territory)
Siobhan Sydney Bell (b. 1789 ~ Shelbyville, Kentucky)

Stefan Hansen (b. 1813 ~ Cheltenham, Missouri)
Kirsten Hansen (b. 1820 ~ Cheltenham, Missouri)
Leif Fredericksen Hansen (b. 1809 ~ Christiania, Norway)

***

*Hollis McKenna Hansen (b. Sparta, Wisconsin)

Kris Tualla is a dynamic, award-winning, and internationally published author of historical romance and suspense. She started in 2006 with nothing but a nugget of a character in mind, and has created a dynasty with The Hansen Series, and its spin-off, The Discreet Gentleman Series. Find out more at: www.KrisTualla.com

Kris is an active PAN member of Romance Writers of America, the Historical Novel Society, and Sisters in Crime, and was invited to be a guest instructor at the Piper Writing Center at Arizona State University. An enthusiastic speaker and teacher, Kris co-created *The Dreams Convention*—combining Arizona's only romance reader event: ArizonaDreaminEvent.com and its author-focused companion: BuildintheDream.com.

*"In the Historical Romance genre, there have been countless kilted warrior stories told. I say it's time for a new breed of heroes. Come along with me and find out why: **Norway IS the new Scotland!**"*

Made in the USA
Charleston, SC
20 March 2016